fifteen
love

For Kate

fifteen love

Robert Corbet

Walker & Company
New York

First published in 2001 as *Fifteen Love* in Australia by Allen & Unwin, 83 Alexander Street, Crows Nest, Sydney, NSW 2065; first published in the United States of America in 2003 by Walker Publishing Company, Inc.; first paperback edition published in 2005.

Published simultaneously in Canada by Fitzhenry and Whiteside, Markham, Ontario L3R 4T8

For information about permission to reproduce selections from this book, write to Permissions, Walker & Company, 104 Fifth Avenue, New York, New York 10011

Library of Congress Cataloging-in-Publication Data
Corbet, Robert.
    Fifteen love / Robert Corbet.
      p. cm.
    Originally published: Sydney, N.S.W.: Allen & Unwin, 2001.
    Summary: Mia, a violist, and Will, a tennis player, each relate their feelings about each other, school, friends, and family troubles as they struggle to understand the opposite sex and to survive being fifteen.
    ISBN 0-8027-8851-3
    [1. Interpersonal relations—Fiction.   2. Family problems—Fiction.
3. Musicians—Fiction.   4. Tennis—Fiction.   5. Australia—Fiction.]   I. Title.
PZ7.C7983 Fi 2003
[Fic]—dc21

                                        2002031146
ISBN 0-8027-7714-7 (paperback)

Book design by Andrew Cunningham-Studio Pazzo

Visit Walker & Company's Web site at www.walkeryoungreaders.com

Printed in the United States of America

10 9 8 7 6 5 4 3 2 1

b169934350

Acknowledgments

Thanks to Elly for the opening serve;
to Julia, who knew about ironing hair;
to Stevie the walking encyclopedia;
to Michael for the viola lesson;
to Bugs, who saved the computer;
and to Sarah, Eva, and Rosalind, who
made the line calls.

one

Mia

Boys are immature. They only use 1 percent of their brain. They only ever talk about cars or sports. They only ever think about sex. I read somewhere that boys think about sex—on average—once every fifteen seconds! That's four times a minute! Two hundred and forty times per hour! I checked on my calculator—it's a total of five thousand, seven hundred, and sixty times a day, assuming boys also dream about sex. . . . If this is true, it is *a real worry*. Fifteen seconds is barely enough time to say hello. No wonder boys never make any sense when you talk to them.

There is one boy at our school who is not like the others. Will Holland definitely has something on his mind. Most lunchtimes he sits alone on the grass, wearing a tracksuit and looking very out of place. He eats his lunch, then he lies back on the grass, staring up at the sky for ages and ages. What does he see up there? What does he think about?

Is he interested in meteorology?

Is he worried about global warming?

Is he watching out for UFOs?

Will Holland is a mystery. My friends say he's either an escaped criminal or else he's suffering from some incurable, highly infectious disease. They think just because Will doesn't hang out with other boys, he must be hiding something. But I think he's interesting. I mean, boys don't *have* to play basketball, do they? They don't *have* to be nerds who lust after computer-generated sex goddesses with breasts made of high-density steel, and slobber uncontrollably whenever a real girl walks past. Do they?

Will Holland isn't like that. I'm sure he has other things on his mind. I swear, even if I had a figure like Lara Croft, he wouldn't even notice me.

Will

Mia Foley is not as pretty as she thinks she is. Without her long, dark hair—which she keeps swishing around as if she's in some kind of shampoo commercial—she would be quite average-looking. Without her big brown eyes and long lashes, her smooth white skin and rosy red lips, her beautiful smile and her perfect teeth, Mia Foley would be very ordinary.

Every lunchtime she and her friends sit together on their seat. Every lunchtime it's the exact same seat, as if there's a plaque that says "Reserved for Mia Foley and her two bimbo buddies," then below in small print, "Boys, please line up and wait your turn." Every day I see new boys come along to try out. They stand there with their hands in their pockets, pretending it's all very casual, when really they're pumped up and trying to make an impression. Then the hands come out of the pockets and the circus starts:

Roll up! Roll up! Pre-senting the a-mazing, the a-stounding, the death-defying des-per-adoes! They juggle! They swing! They spin basketballs on their fingertips! They throw things! They fight! Just sit back and enjoy the show, ladies, until the tightrope walker falls flat on his face and the clowns come to take him away.

Mia and her friends like the attention. They smile and laugh, but they never ask the boys to sit down and join them. In the end, their eyes start to glaze over, and it's time for the circus to pack up and leave.

When the boys have gone, the girls huddle together and talk in low voices.

I have no idea what they talk about.

I wish I were a fly on the wall.

I wish I had a tape recorder and a hidden microphone. . . .

Mia

"The tracksuit is watching you again," says Renata.

"No, he isn't."

"Mia! Are you blind?" says Vanessa.

"Just nearsighted, remember?"

"Is he that guy you said was kind of cute?" says Renata.

"I never said that."

"He's okay-looking. I'd lose the tracksuit, though," says Vanessa.

"Lose it? He lives in it. I don't think he owns any other clothes," says Renata.

"Pee-ew! Stinky!" says Vanessa.

"Give him a break."

"I mean, a tracksuit is for inside the house, right?" says Renata.

"I've heard some people do *actually* play sports in them," says Vanessa.

"I think he wears a *tennis* shirt underneath," says Renata.

"That's a worry," says Vanessa.

"Maybe he's trying to get in the *Guinness Book of World Records*," says Renata.

"Will Holland, record holder for the world's stinkiest tracksuit!" says Vanessa.

Vanessa and Renata are my two best friends. We share our lunches. We share our tampons. And we share our troubles. Mostly, our troubles are boy troubles, and mostly they're Vanessa's boy troubles, because it's Vanessa the boys are mostly interested in.

Vanessa is a big flirt, to put it politely. She wears cardigans that are three sizes too small, just to show off her pierced belly button and so she can push right up close to guys, as if she's trying to pop the buttons. Vanessa has this way of looking at guys that she does without thinking. She does it to guys she's interested in, but she also does it to complete strangers—guys on the train who are ten years older. Hence the boy troubles.

(My mom says I'm allowed to get my belly button pierced, but my dad says I'm not. He says there are "medical reasons," and just because he's a doctor, my mom believes him. The truth is, my father thinks having a pierced belly button is the same as having sex. Diagnosis: AIDS and/or an unwanted pregnancy. But I don't care. One day, I'll just go out and do it anyway—get my belly button pierced, I mean.)

Vanessa has two kinds of boy troubles. Either it's two guys fighting over her, or else one guy who's been driven to the edge and can't help himself. Renata and I try giving Vanessa a subtle hint. We tell her to tone it down if she wants guys to leave her alone, but then she gets really offended and won't talk to us. Vanessa is unpredictable when it comes to guys. She can spend weeks playing hard to get with a gorgeous boy, then suddenly go out with a serial killer.

Renata is like Vanessa in some ways, but in other ways she's the exact opposite. Renata is just as pretty as Vanessa and goes to the same trouble with her hair, but she's not so confident. Renata is Yugoslavian, and her parents are pretty strict. She's been living here for five years, but she still won't talk about the place where she was born. My dad told me Yugoslavia doesn't exist anymore. It's not a real country, he said. But if anyone ever mentions Yugoslavia—or Serbia, Bosnia, Kosovo, any of those places—Renata goes a bit pale. I think some of her family must have got killed or something.

Renata says Vanessa is good for us. She's always telling us how nice we look and encouraging us to be more up-front with boys. Vanessa is the "in girl" at our school, so there's never any shortage of boys around. The trouble is, boys are always at their silliest whenever they're trying to impress girls.

Will

Thank you for calling Cosmo Girl! *magazine. Please press (1) if you wish to subscribe. Press (2) if you wish to know what girls talk about. Press (3) if you only want to know what "a certain girl" talks about. Press (4) if you really just want to meet "a certain girl," but have no idea how to go about it.*

Should I subscribe to *Cosmo Girl!* magazine? Or should I buy a sample copy first? I could buy it from the supermarket. I could slip it in between the Nutri-Grain and the Granola Crunch, so that no one would even see it.

"It's for my sister," I could say, if anyone asked.

Except that I don't have a sister.

If I subscribed, the magazine would be mailed once a month, hopefully in a plain brown envelope, clearly addressed to me, so that no one else would open it.

Because I do have a brother, and I don't want him getting the wrong idea.

I have heard that parts of *Cosmo Girl!* magazine can be quite intimate. I have heard that the dating sections are extremely intimate! I have glanced at the letters where girls reveal their innermost secrets. I want to know how girls think, but my real reason for buying *Cosmo Girl!* magazine is less sleazy than that. I need *Cosmo Girl!* magazine for research purposes. I need to know what girls talk about. If I'm going to talk to Mia Foley one day, I need to be prepared.

Mia Foley is an up-to-date kind of girl. She dresses like the girls in *Cosmo Girl!* magazine. She is easily beautiful enough to be on the cover of *Cosmo Girl!* magazine. But that doesn't mean Mia actually *reads* it. And besides, *Cosmo Girl!* is a magazine for girls. It's all about what girls say to other girls. It's probably about boys. And if I ever meet Mia Foley, that is one subject we are definitely *not* going to talk about.

The trouble is, when boys talk, we talk about *things*. We exchange information. We are interested in the facts. Girls may not want to know about carburetors or shock-absorbers, but they are impressed by boys who know stuff. Any stuff—magnetic fields, microbiology, hydraulic engineering—it doesn't really matter what. Girls like guys who know stuff. It makes them feel comfortable. They feel like the guy has other interests, that he's not in danger of getting hopelessly obsessed about them. Stalkers, I'll bet, have very little interest in the facts.

If, and hopefully when, I do meet Mia, we should have one of those magical conversations that just click. "What a lovely day," she might say. "Yes," I would reply. "The forecast high temperature is 80 degrees, I believe." "Don't you wish it could always be this nice?" she might say. Then I would explain how the earth tilts on its axis as it moves around the sun, so that the chance of it being 80 degrees and sunny every day is pretty unlikely. "And anyway," we would both agree, "life would be pretty boring without a change of season."

Then Mia might say, "I read in *Cosmo Girl!* magazine how the weather affects what we feel."

"*Cosmo Girl!* magazine?" I would say. "Isn't that mainly for girls?"

Mia

"You did *what?*"I say.

"You did *what?*" says Renata.

Renata and I are shocked and stunned. Vanessa has truly outdone herself this time.

"I sucked his toe," she says.

"His *big* toe?" says Renata.

"Yes," says Vanessa.

"You took off his shoe?" I say.

"Yes," says Vanessa.

"And his sock?" says Renata.

"Of course," says Vanessa.

"Was it clean?" I ask.

"Pretty clean," says Vanessa.

"And what did *he* do, while you were sucking his toe?" says Renata.

"He went a bit crazy," says Vanessa. "He told me he loved me!"

"He *didn't!*" I say.

"But he's not even your boyfriend!" says Renata.

Vanessa hides her face in her hands. "He is now," she says, softly.

I shake my head in disbelief. Renata can't stop laughing. She has tears running down her cheeks and cramps in her stomach. There is something not quite right about the way Renata is laughing. In fact, there is something deeply disturbing about it.

Vanessa and Renata are my two best friends, but even

best friends can be weird sometimes. Sucking boys' toes isn't something I want to leap into, I must admit. It might sound old-fashioned, but toe-sucking isn't something I want to rush right into. It's not something I would ever do on a first date. It's not my idea of romance. If you ask me, toe-sucking is something that should happen much later. It's something a girl should only do with someone she really loves, and only after he's had a long, soapy bath.

Will

It all started in woodshop. The teacher wasn't there yet, and my workbench was the only one with an empty seat. I was minding my own business—crushing my pencil in my vise—when in walked The Most Beautiful Girl in the Whole Wide World. There are beautiful girls in movies and in magazines, but this girl was something else. She was real! And she was coming straight at me!

The Most Beautiful Girl in the Whole Wide World sat down beside me at my workbench, as my pencil cracked loudly up the middle. She looked at me, then at my pencil. I was stumped. I didn't know what to say.

On the back of her hand she had written, *"Don't forget V!"* in red ballpoint.

Don't forget V!??—I have never seen anything so mysterious and exotic in all my life. But before I had any time to think about what *V* was, before I could think of anything to say, Mia had put on her glasses and realized where she was.

"Whoops!" she said. "Wrong room!" Then she stood up and walked out.

That was it. Forget about *V*. The Most Beautiful Girl in the Whole Wide World was gone. V for *Vanished*. When I looked at her seat, I wanted to reach across and touch it, to run my fingers across the smooth, polished wood. It was all I had left.

V for *Vacant?* . . . *Vacuum?* . . . *Vapor?* . . .

It ruined my whole day. Actually, it was longer than that. Woodworking was tragic for at least another month. I made a pencil box and filled it full of broken pencils. The empty seat stayed empty, but I couldn't give up hope that Mia might make the same mistake again. I imagined she might come in and sit down on her seat again, just for old times' sake. So I guarded it, just in case.

"Is that seat taken?"

"Yeah. She'll be back soon."

Who was I kidding? Mia was never coming back.

V for *Venus* . . . *Velvet* . . . *Visitor* . . .

I started checking the schedule after that, to see where Mia's classes were. Without really meaning to, I started wandering past her classrooms just to sneak a glance at her. It sounds like something a psychopath would do, I know, but I couldn't help it. And every time I saw Mia, she looked even more beautiful than I remembered. Her hair was more shiny, her face was more perfect. Until, one day, Mia looked up and saw me staring at her. I tried to smile, but she acted like she didn't even know me.

That's because she didn't even know me.

V for *Victim* . . . *V* for *Vegetable* . . .

After that, I gave up spying on Mia in class, but lunchtimes weren't so easy. I tried to act normal and just do the things you normally do, but out of the corner of my eye I was always looking out for her. If I ever did see her, or even someone *who might have been* her, my body felt like a robot being operated by remote control. My limbs would move in unexpected ways. My eyelids would twitch, and my neck muscles would go into spasm. I have to admit it— I had a slight problem with Mia Foley.

WHO CAN YOU TURN TO? said the poster on the library window.

The school counseling service is available for students who:
  • *are having difficulty making friends*
  • *are experiencing disruptions in their personal lives*
  • *are having trouble studying*
  • *are uncertain about their future*

The school counselor, as it turned out, was also the music teacher. I don't know if Ms. Stanway had any counseling qualifications, but there's obviously a connection between psychos and music—just look at Marilyn Manson. It didn't matter, though, because from the moment I sat down in Ms. Stanway's big comfy chair, I knew I couldn't say I was there because of a *girl*.

"It's spiders," I said, instead. "They make me feel . . . anxious."

Ms. Stanway had long white fingers with pale pink nails. She pressed her index finger to her chin, as if she were trying to make a dimple.

"How do you mean, exactly?"

"Whenever I see her coming—the spider, that is—I have to walk away."

"Arachnophobia." Ms. Stanway nodded. "It's quite common."

"Actually," I said. "It's more like an obsession than a phobia. I keep expecting her—it!—to appear from out of nowhere. I don't know what I would do if it suddenly tapped me on the shoulder and said, 'Hi.'"

Ms. Stanway's finger started making a circular motion, as if it were trying to rub out the dimple. "Obsessions," she said, "are sometimes like phobias, and phobias often occur as the result of uncertainty or unfamiliarity. Often, when you have a phobia, it's best to confront the thing you are scared of, face-to-face. If it is spiders, say, you could keep one in a jar on your desk. You should try to transform them from something terrifying into something familiar, if—as you say—it's spiders that you're scared of."

"Jar on the desk," I nodded. "Not a problem!"

Ms. Stanway's fingers joined to make a white church with a pale pink roof.

"Of course, if it were something else—a girl, for instance—then the same principle would apply."

I wasn't quite ready to *meet* Mia Foley yet, so I opted for the jar on the desk instead. I would have had trouble finding a jar that was big enough, of course, so the only other way of not being anxious was to keep Mia under observation at all times.

That first lunchtime when I started watching her, I felt sick to my stomach. My skin prickled with sweat. If Mia looked in my direction, I had to look away. If she stood up suddenly, I had a desperate urge to run and hide in the Dumpster, to wait for the truck to come and take me away.

Maybe that's why they call it a crush.

Gradually, day by day, it got better. It wasn't long before I could eat my lunch in front of her. I could turn my back on her. I could lie down, defenseless, staring up at the sky. I could almost forget her, unless there were clouds shaped like angels.

V for *Volleyball?* . . . *Vitamins?* . . . *Video?* . . . *Vanilla?*

I was making good progress, until one day I overheard some guys talking about who were the top ten biggest babes in our class. They all agreed on Vanessa and Renata, but Mia's name didn't even come up! I sat and listened for ten whole minutes, until I figured they must have just forgotten about her.

"What about Mia Foley?" I said casually. "She's a bit of a babe, isn't she?"

"Four-eyes Foley!" They all laughed. "She's a stick! A scrawny little chicken."

Maybe it wasn't a phobia or even an obsession. Maybe I just needed glasses.

Mia

As soon as she hears the front door open, Harriet starts whining and scratching at the back door. When I let her into the house, she tears up and down the hall, slipping on the polished floorboards as she runs from room to room.

"Hello, girl! Did you miss me?"

As an answer, Harriet leaps kamikaze-style at my face, smashing into my jaw and almost knocking herself out as she tries to lick me.

"Down, girl! Down!"

Harriet was my birthday present. She's a purebred beagle—white, tan, and black—with big, loving eyes, saggy-baggy skin, soft, floppy ears, and long, white socks. Technically, Harriet is no longer a puppy, but sometimes I wonder if she will ever grow up. People say beagles are smart in packs, but stupid on their own. Harriet has already flunked two obedience schools. At six months old she still can't be let off her leash. I don't have any brothers or sisters, so for years and years I wanted a dog. By the time I got Harriet, she was more like a reckless toddler than a substitute sister.

"Walk, girl?"

I slip on Harriet's leash, and we go to the park. I tell her to stay by my side, but she's too busy sniffing at trees and fences to take any notice. At the airport they use beagles as sniffer dogs because of their excellent noses, so Harriet is in her element, searching relentlessly for doggy trails and illegal substances.

Harriet and I sit by the lake to watch the ducks. The ducks know that Harriet is too young and silly to be any real threat. Harriet sits when I say "Sit!" and lies when I say "Lie down." But she soon forgets and is up and tugging on her leash again, ready to go.

If I had a boyfriend, I'm sure Harriet would be jealous. She wouldn't let us sit alone by the lake. If we held hands, I'm sure she would leap into the water and attack the ducks, just to embarrass me. If I had a boyfriend . . . How can I contemplate having a boyfriend when I can't even teach my own dog to stay?

Will

Imaginary Conversation # 216:

"Thanks for the flowers," Mia would say. "They were *so beautiful!*"

And I would say, "It's hard to believe the whole point of flowers is to attract bees."

And Mia would say, "Do you think that bees know how beautiful flowers are?"

"Maybe they do," I would say. "After all, bees are very intelligent creatures."

"Bees are very mysterious," Mia would say. "Who knows what they think?"

And I would say, "Did you know that they navigate by the angle of the sun?"

"Yes," Mia would say. "And they communicate by dancing."

"Bees are very mysterious," I would say.

"Did you know," Mia would say, "that all the worker bees are female?"

"Very mysterious," I would say. "Who knows what they think?"

Mia

The truth is, falling in love is not high on my list of priorities right now. I have books to read and homework to do. I have Harriet to look after and orchestra practice twice a week. I don't have the time to fall in love, and I don't have the right clothes. To have a boyfriend, you need clothes for every occasion. One day you might get invited to the movies, then the next you might get asked to go ice-skating. I have nothing to wear to a party. I can't imagine what I'd wear to go skydiving.

Having a boyfriend means going places you've never been before. It means doing things you don't want to do, like sucking toes and jumping out of airplanes. I swear, I'm not ready for that kind of adventurous lifestyle.

Will

I have discovered "V"! I have seen Mia Foley walking across the schoolyard, and in her hand she was carrying a violin case. V is for Violin! V is for Victory!

Because of this, I have a whole new range of options.

a. Walk up to Mia and say, "It's good to see you remembered your violin today. Remember me? The guy with the broken pencil?"

b. Steal Mia's violin and deliver a ransom note:

"Marry me, or else the violin gets it!"

c. Plan an accidental, violin-related meeting.

Most days, Mia Foley is like a maximum-security facility. Every recess and lunchtime she sits on the same bench, guarded by her two wardens. Except on Mondays and Thursdays, when Mia goes down to the music room to rehearse with the school orchestra. Only the musicians are allowed in there, but I could go along, just to make a few inquiries. I might even say I'm interested in playing the triangle. I mean, how difficult can it be to ting on a triangle when the conductor gives you the nod?

In preparation, I go to the library and borrow a book called *The Orchestra*. There's plenty about violins and not much on triangles, so I brush up on my basic musical terminology (notes, chords, time signatures, etc.), just to be on the safe side. But musical theory isn't really my scene. If Mia puts me on the spot, I will tell her I have a jazz background, and that history is full of gifted triangle players who play by ear.

Mia

What, in the name of Wolfgang Amadeus Mozart, is Will Holland doing here? Shouldn't he be outside on the grass?

Did something fall from the sky and hit him on the head? Surely he's not going to audition? What instrument does he play? Does he realize how surly Ms. S. can be? No one has *ever* turned up at rehearsal in a tracksuit before. I can't bear to watch. . . .

Will

Ms. Stanway opens the door to the room where the orchestra is tuning up. If she hadn't already talked to me about arachnophobia, I'm sure Ms. Stanway would have turned me away. Instead, she gives me a knowing look and invites me in.

When I tell her I want to audition, she looks skeptical.

"Can you read?" she asks.

"Of course," I reply, showing her my library book.

Ms. Stanway frowns and shows me a book of sheet music: *The Four Seasons* by Antonio Vivaldi. "Can you read *music?*" she asks. "Can you read *timpani?*"

"Timpani? Hmm . . . I'm familiar with *some* of his work."

Ms. Stanway wags a long finger at me. "There's more to playing percussion than just banging a few drums," she says. "You can sit beside Allan and watch, if you like."

I'm in!

Allan is way over in the corner, about as far from the violins as you can get, surrounded by all kinds of junk. There are xylophones and glockenspiels, glockenphones and xylospiels, but no triangles. Allan is a weedy guy to look at, but he can do an excellent drum roll with his big, fluffy sticks: *brrrrrdummm . . . brrrrrrdummm . . .*

The orchestra tunes up, and on the count of four they rip into *Autumn*. It's all very windy and swirly as Ms. Stanway bends and sways like an old elm tree, lifting up her arms and calling out in Italian: "Allegro! More allegro!"

I stand to the side, trying to look like Allan's drum roadie, when really I'm watching Mia. She's wearing glasses that make her look unbelievably cool, and the way her fingers slide up and down the neck of the violin is deeply disturbing. Trying not to be noticed, I inch myself slowly along the wall, hoping to get a better view of her.

In the second part of *Autumn*, the music slows right down, and the wind instruments take over. I imagine Mia being buried under a pile of fallen leaves. I imagine getting one of those industrial-strength vacuum cleaners that gardeners use and sucking all the leaves off, until she's just lying there on the grass. I can't help it. It's in the music.

All of a sudden Mia looks up and smiles at me. It gives me such a shock, my foot kicks over a cymbal that is leaning against the wall. It falls with an almighty *crash!* and everyone looks at me. Mia laughs, and Ms. Stanway points to the door, with a frown that says, Take your spiders and leave!

As I stumble out of the room, Mia smiles and sneaks me a good-bye wave.

It makes me so happy, I turn like a conductor to take my final bow.

Mia

Vanessa and Renata *tolerate* me playing in the school orchestra. They don't mind me talking about classical music, and sometimes they even ask questions about it. But Vanessa and Renata don't listen to classical music. They don't own any classical CDs.

"Classical music is for dead people," Vanessa says. "All those decomposing composers." Vanessa's taste in music is strictly twenty-first century. She listens to KPOP, and she buys top-ten singles. Punk, funk, rock, grunge, metal, hip-hop, rap, soul. It doesn't matter to Vanessa, provided it's top ten.

Renata is more complicated. Renata won't actually say what she likes, in case Vanessa thinks it's stupid. For example, I *know* Renata likes K****. I'm sure she has some of K****'s albums—maybe even all of them—and when K**** did her concert, I'm pretty sure Renata went, although she never mentioned it.

"Why is K**** so popular, anyway?" says Vanessa. "She can't sing or dance, and her songs are *so* forgettable."

"She's stylish, though," I say, seeing the disappointment in Renata's face.

"K**** *is* beautiful," says Renata. "Don't you think?"

But Vanessa's response is swift and severe.

"Yes, Renata, and I'm *sure* she's a very nice person."

If Will Holland came to watch our orchestra rehearse, he must know something about music. Ms. S. seemed to know who he was. Maybe he's writing an article for the local paper? Or maybe he's a talent scout, on the lookout for gifted musicians?

Will

These are my remaining options.

a. *Start up my own orchestra and ask Mia to join (any instrument she likes).*

b. *Start up a string quartet (might be easier).*

c. *Pies in the face, buckets of water, exploding cigars, or other attention-seeking devices.*

d. *Get down on my knees and beg.*

e. *Go and talk to her RIGHT NOW!*

Mia

The lunch bell has gone off, and I am late for class. The corridor is full of kids lining up outside classrooms or hurrying to get books from their lockers. When I put on my glasses, I look up and see Will Holland coming straight toward me! We are on a collision course, being pulled along in the current. Then suddenly there we are, face-to-face, blocking each other's way. Will looks like he wants to say something. He opens his mouth, but no words come out.

Will smiles like he's just had his wisdom teeth pulled, top and bottom.

I smile back, helplessly.

What in the name of Marcel Marceau is happening?

Will and I stand there without moving, for what seems like a lifetime, an era, an eon, an ice age. Then I step to the right. At the exact same moment Will steps to the left, so there we are, blocking each other's way again. To correct the mistake we both step back to the center, like in a barn dance. It feels as though we should clap hands and do-si-do. It's ridiculous, but neither of us is laughing.

"Stay there," I say. "Don't move, okay?"

I don't mean to sound rude. It just slips out.

Will stands still as a lamppost while I step past him and walk off down the hall.

I don't want to look back. It is already far too complicated.

Will

If my life was a video, I would rewind to my meeting with Mia Foley in the corridor. I would pause it there, just to see her perfect face again in close-up, then I'd roll it in super-slow motion, taking it one frame at a time. And this time we wouldn't be stuck for words.

"They need a line down the middle," I might say.

"With a sign saying, Keep Left Unless Passing," she'd reply.

"And double lines on the dangerous corners."

"Slippery When Wet," she'd say.

No . . . Pause . . . Rewind . . . Mia definitely wouldn't say that.

"Form One Lane, above the doorway," she'd say.

"Form One Planet, it could say, if you add a P and a T."

Mia would think about this and decide it was very profound.

"Kiss me," she'd say. . . .

Stop the tape. Rewind, erase, and eject. Then stick it in the microwave till it melts to a stinky black blob.

Who am I kidding?

Mia

When I get home from school, I practice my viola. I start with my scales, playing them lento, slowly, then faster, marcato, before moving on to the Vivaldi. There are some days when I'd rather be vegging out in front of the TV. But mostly, once I've started, playing the viola helps my thoughts to unravel. . . .

My bedroom is nowhere near ready for a boyfriend. The wallpaper, for instance, has *pink flowers* on it. My bedspread has daisy chains! There are lace curtains and a chandelier with fake plastic candles! My bedroom looks like a doll's house. It's too *nice* for a boyfriend. In fact, the whole house is too nice. My parents are too nice. Before I even *imagine* having a boyfriend, I would need to paint my room a strong, serious color, possibly indigo. I would need heavy curtains—possibly magenta—plus a matching comforter and a dimmer switch. I would need a queen-size bed, with a new mattress—one that's not quite so loud and boingy.

And I would definitely need a lock on the door—to keep out my nice mom and dad, and my mad, slobbering beagle.

Today, in the library, I saw Will again. He had taken time out from watching the sky to borrow a book. Was this an improvement or a backward step? I wondered. Did it make him more mysterious or less? I guess that depends on the book. From where I was standing, I couldn't see the cover. It was a big, thick hardcover, and Will put it straight into his bag as if he didn't want anyone to see. It could have been about Shakespeare or Baroque musicians or Renaissance art. It definitely looked like the kind of book to make a guy more deep and interesting.

I shouldn't have been so abrupt in the hallway yesterday, telling Will to stand still while I walked around him. Obviously, Will is the kind of boy who takes time to assemble his thoughts. Because his thoughts are so deep and meaningful, he has trouble with "Hello, how are you?"

I should have walked up to Will and asked him what his book was. Will and I need to talk. What about, exactly, I don't know. How, when, and where, I'm not sure. Mainly, we need to talk so that we can stop being so ridiculous. It doesn't look like Will is going to make the first move, so I guess it's up to me.

And maybe I should brush up on my Shakespeare, just to be on the safe side.

Will

I am walking out the school gate when I almost collide with Mia Foley again! I am stunned. Here we both are, with the entire school ground to move around in, and yet we keep on crashing into each other. Mia and I are like bumper cars or billiard balls. We couldn't avoid each other, even if we tried.

"Hi!" she says, as if our meeting in the hall had never happened.

"Hi," I say, hoping for something with a bit more oomph! "Hello!"

"Hello," Mia replies.

So far, so good.

Safely through the gate, Mia and I drift along the sidewalk together. I'm not about to tell her my house is in the opposite direction. Instead, I stumble along, putting one foot in front of the other and trying to work out what to say next, hoping to capitalize on "Hello." Then I have a brain wave. Of course! How obvious! It was right there in front of me all along. *Don't forget V!*

Casually, I point to the case she is carrying. "Is that your violin?"

"No," she says. "It's my machine gun."

"Silly question, I guess."

"Actually, it's a viola."

"Ah!" I say, hopelessly faking it.

"What's the difference between a violin and a viola?" Mia asks.

This seems like a very unfair question to me. After all, it's not a TV quiz show.

"Um . . ."

"You can tune a violin," she says.

I nod uncertainly.

"It's a joke," says Mia. "What's the difference between a violin and a viola? A viola burns longer. . . . How do you keep your violin from getting stolen? Put it in a viola case. People are always making jokes about violas."

I don't know whether to feel stupid or relieved. "How come?"

"Violas are weird," says Mia. "They're either too small to get a good sound, or too big to fit under your chin. Really, they should be played on your knee—viola da gamba style. Also, music for viola is written in the alto clef, which most conductors can't read and most composers can't be bothered writing for. Violins rule. Violas don't get many solos, even though Beethoven and Mozart both played the viola. . . . Sorry, I'm talking too much."

"Can I have a look at it?"

Mia looks at me suspiciously. "If you like."

We stop walking. Mia opens the case and takes out the viola. It's a beautiful instrument, with its solid curves and tiger-striped wood grain.

"It's a really old one," she says. "My dad used to play it when he was at school. It was made in Italy. It needs a bit of work, but it's probably worth a fortune."

Mia takes out the bow, tightens it, and brushes on some

rosin. She picks up the viola and tucks it under her chin, plucking the strings and adjusting the pegs, then bowing the strings in pairs to check the tuning. She plays a simple melody, and the instrument comes alive with beautiful sound. The tone is like a violin's, only darker and richer, like chocolate. It gives me goose bumps. When she finishes playing, I am speechless. I don't know whether to applaud or not.

Mia

I finish playing, and Will just stands there, looking uncertain. I pack away the viola, then to cover up my embarrassment, I change the subject.

"Anyway," I ask, "what's that book you got out of the library today?"

Will looks worried. "It's just a book."

"It's not Shakespeare, is it?"

"Who? William Shakespeare?"

"No, Freddie—his brother."

"It's not the complete works of Freddie Shakespeare, no."

"Aren't you going to tell me?"

"Do I have to?"

"I showed you my viola."

"But what if you think it's stupid?"

"I probably haven't even read it."

"You *definitely* haven't read it."

"It's not the Bible, is it?"

"No, and it's not the Koran, either."

"Then just *show* me!"

Will Holland—literary enigma and mystical sky-gazer—fishes around in his bag and reluctantly brings out his big book. At last, the moment of truth . . .

The Encyclopedia of Tennis, it says on the cover.

I take the book and open it. Inside, there's a photo of a woman called Doris and a whole lot of dates and statistics.

"It's . . . not what I expected."

Trying hard not to look disappointed, I close the book and hand it back to Will.

"It's for my brother," he says. "No, really. It is."

Will puts the book away, and we walk on in silence. How could I have been so stupid? Will Holland is not a journalist or a talent scout. The reason why Will wears a tennis shirt underneath his tracksuit is that he *plays tennis.* The reason why he lies out on the grass at lunchtime is that he's so *exhausted* from playing tennis. The reason he doesn't say much is that he'd rather be *playing tennis!* I feel stupid for having talked so much about things that Will must think are so boring. Stupid, that I showed him my viola and made him listen to me play it! No wonder he didn't say anything. I swear, he must think I am such an idiot!

When we get to my street, I say good-bye.

"That's my house over there," I point. "Behind the big brick wall."

Will

Thank you for calling Men Who Can't Speak. We have placed you in a very long line. Do you really have anything to say to us? Shouldn't you just hang up right now?

As I look to where Mia is pointing, a man steps into the street and opens the car door.

"It's my dad!" she says. "Quick! I don't want him to see us."

Mia and I retreat into a driveway. As the car goes past I see a middle-aged man and a younger woman with blond hair and red lipstick. The man smiles at the girl, and she smiles back at him. She flicks back her hair, then they're gone.

When I look back at Mia, her face has gone pale.

"Is that your sister?"

"I don't have a sister," she says.

Mia

Instead of letting Harriet in, I go to my bedroom and close the door. I take out my viola and start practicing, but it's hard to concentrate. The notes seem to be moving around on the page, and my fingers won't go where I want them to. No matter what I do, my viola still sounds out of tune. The open strings sound fine in pairs, but the top A string is out with the bottom C.

If only my bedroom were more adult-looking. It's impossible to think like an adult in a room that keeps on insisting you're ten years old. What I need is a new set of posters. Scenes from a rain forest, maybe, to help clear my head and calm my thoughts. Harriet is scratching the back door down. There is no need to panic, Harriet! Do not jump to conclusions! There is a simple explanation for everything.

And by far the simplest explanation is that my father is having an affair with a woman half his age!

My mom and dad aren't exactly the most romantic couple in the world, but then they *have* been married for sixteen-odd years. Dad often works late and takes patients after hours. The girl in his car was a nurse. Dad works in a hospital. He borrowed a nurse and then came home to pick up his stethoscope. There's always a simple explanation.

Then why was she wearing red lipstick?

I close my viola book and try to comfort myself with a simple melody in the key of C, while outside my window Harriet continues to whine and bark: *Do, a deer, a female deer . . . Re, a drop of golden sun . . . Me, a name I call my-self . . .* I wish I wasn't me. I wish I was Julie Andrews in *The Sound of Music*. I wish I could climb the monastery walls and escape into the Alps . . . *Fa, a long long way to run . . .*

Will

The next day, after school, Mia is waiting at the gate for me.

"We need to talk," she says urgently. "It's about what happened yesterday."

"If you want to borrow *The Encyclopedia of Tennis,* you'll have to wait."

Mia frowns. "What you saw—my father and that girl—it's not what you think."

"You mean, she's not his girlfriend?"

"Don't even *say that word*! I want you to promise not to tell anyone."

"But I thought you said—"

"You have to promise *never* to tell another living soul."

"I promise."

"*Especially* not my friends, okay?"

"I promise not to tell a single soul, especially not your friends."

"But how do I know I can trust you?"

"You could hypnotize me. All you need is a watch on a chain."

But Mia isn't laughing.

"*Please!*" she says. "Just forget it ever happened."

two

Mia

"I'm fat!" says Renata.

"No, you're not!" say Vanessa and I.

"Yes, I am. I'm a big fat pig!"

"Renata! You're gorgeous!"

The school dance is only two days away, so the three of us are desperately shopping. We are in *T——* for the Twenty Percent Off Footwear and Clothing Sale. The reason I can't say the name of the store is because Vanessa says it's humiliating. Normally, Vanessa wouldn't be caught dead in *T——*, but because of the Twenty Percent Off Sale, she's decided to compromise.

"The labels will come off easily enough," she says. "But no one must *ever* find out!"

We are in the changing rooms, and Vanessa is lying on the floor, squirming around like a squashed lizard, trying desperately to pull on her stretch denim jeans. Renata and I are supposed to be trying on bras, but we've been distracted by the size of our butts in the full-length mirror.

"Cellulite at fifteen. How humiliating!"

"Renata!"

"Oh, well, time to start saving for liposuction."

Buying a bra is one of those things you can't afford to skimp on, even at 20 percent off. Bras are more than just underwear. The bra you choose determines the shape of your boobs. And according to Vanessa, the shape of your boobs determines everything else. A bra has to feel right, look right, and send off the right signals.

"You want to generate interest," Vanessa says, "without getting slobbered over."

Vanessa and Renata are both 34Cs, which is pretty much ideal in terms of bra sizes. I'm a 34B, but I'm hoping my boobs haven't stopped growing yet. I'm worried that certain foods might affect breast size. I tried exercising, but then I read somewhere that too much exercise can actually decrease breast growth. Vanessa says that when she was a 34B she used padding and upgraded to a 34C, but she had to keep checking that the pads were still in place. Being caught with your hands inside your bra is *not* a good look.

Do boys all prefer 34Cs, I wonder? Or are 34Bs seen as having potential? Do boys want girls who look like models or porn stars? And do girls really care what boys like?

Renata and I wear regular sports bras, but Vanessa has a bra for every occasion. She has black lacy ones, plunging ones, see-through, boob tubes, strapless, you name it. (She has silky ones for special occasions—guaranteed to make her nipples show—and she desperately wants one of those pump-up Wonder Bras, for extra cleavage.) Vanessa can get away with stuff like that. She knows she's got a great body. She has that model's way of walking, where she holds her head up and pulls back her arms until her shoulder blades are almost touching. Vanessa wants to be a model, and she's the kind of girl who can pull it off. She's confident, sexy, and she knows how to smile.

With most of the button fly done up, Vanessa drags herself into a standing position and starts checking herself out from every conceivable angle, doing every conceivable thing with her butt. After a long discussion, she decides to "maybe not buy them," if she can get them off again.

Between the two of them, I swear, Vanessa and Renata have tried every diet on the planet: the low-carb diet, the low-fat diet, the low-calorie diet, the liver-cleansing diet, the snack diet, the no-snack diet, the all-greens diet, the all-yellows diet. Vanessa went vegetarian for a month. She even tried going macrobiotic for an hour, but all that chewing made her jaws cramp. These days Vanessa prefers what she calls the "supermodel's diet." She eats what she likes, then she goes to the toilet and sticks her fingers down her throat.

"It feels really good," she says. "Like cheating and getting away with it."

If you ask me, it's disgusting. In fact, the best advice I ever heard for losing weight is: Eat less. There are fewer calories in a single scoop of extra creamy ice cream than a bucket of low-fat goo.

Vanessa is on the floor again now, keeping her butt in the air while Renata and I take hold of one leg each. We're rolling around laughing when suddenly a giant shadow looms in the doorway. It's the dragon lady—the changing room attendant—and she is not smiling.

"What do you think this is," she says, wagging her finger at us. "A children's playground?"

Vanessa smiles her "up-yours" smile.

"Yes," she says. "And you are a child molester."

Will

There's only one place to get your hair cut, and that's Mondo for Men. Two guys work there, Matteo and Ricardo. Matteo is an artist—he does exactly what you say. Ricki is a madman—a danger to society.

Most guys won't admit it, but getting a haircut can be a bit tense. You have to trust the guy to do what you say, so you have to say what you want. It has to sound casual and unimportant, but clear and unambiguous: "Just a trim, thanks." I practice it going to sleep, then in the shower, over breakfast, and finally, on the bus. "Just a trim, thanks . . . Just a trim, thanks . . ." It's best to be prepared.

I enter Mondo for Men and proceed to the plush leather couch with the men's magazines on the tinted glass coffee table. I wait my turn, watching Matteo and Ricki, trying to predict who I'll get. Ricki is faster than Matteo. Matteo is a perfectionist, whereas Ricki is more like a shearer, racing against the clock. He'll take the guy before me, meaning I will get Matt. Not a problem. Just a trim, thanks.

I open a magazine and start flipping through the pages. There's an article about how to deal with stress. You have to block out what's going on around you, it says. You have to learn to focus on the task at hand. . . .

"Next?"

With my head in the magazine, I hear the voice of doom above me. Ricki has already finished, and I'm next in line. I could let someone go ahead of me and say I'm waiting for Matt. I could get up and run from the room.

"How you doin', all right?"

"Just a trim, thanks."

Nervously, I climb into the chair. Ricki clips a smock around my neck and tries to choke me with paper towels. He is too busy talking to Matteo to notice how uncomfortable I am: "She was comin' on real strong, but she was keepin' her distance, you know what I mean? She was hot, but she was cool, too, you know what I mean?"

I sit watching helplessly as Ricardo goes to work. He starts with his scissors and a fine-toothed comb that he digs into my scalp. The scissors snip around my head at lightning speed. I'm sure he'll nip off a piece of my ear, but I'm more worried about my hair. Do I need to repeat the instructions, just in case?

To calm my nerves I start whispering, "Just a trim, thanks . . . Just a trim, thanks."

Good news. Ricardo has put away the scissors and picked up the electric shears. My hair looks okay. Shorter than I'd wanted, but okay. Good enough. Ricardo trims the hairs on the back of my neck. He's finishing up. I'm almost in the clear. He neatens the sides, but then, before I know it, he's shaving up and around my ears! I feel the buzz of the shears against my skull. Ricardo is giving me a mohawk!

. . . Just a trim, thanks . . . Just a trim, thanks . . .

In desperation, I try tilting my head away, but Ricardo simply pushes it back up again.

"What do you think?" he asks when he's done.

I nod, and in the mirror the guy with the brain-surgery haircut nods grimly back at me.

Mia

"I hate my hair!"

"Mia! You don't mean that."

"Yes I do. It's driving me crazy. I feel like getting it all cut off."

Vanessa looks horrified. "Don't even joke about it. You have gorgeous hair!"

Renata agrees. "I wish I had your hair, Mia."

"It's all dry and frizzy. This morning when I woke up, there were at least five strands on my pillow! I swear, I'm going bald!"

"Mushrooms," says Vanessa. "You have to eat more mushrooms."

"I don't like mushrooms. Do you know where those things are grown?"

"How about wheat germ and honey, as a conditioner?"

"Sure. So I wake up screaming in the night, being attacked by a swarm of ants."

"Eggs."

"Too stinky."

"Tofu."

"Tofu?"

"Yeah. I'm not sure what you're meant to do with it, though."

I am kneeling beside the ironing board while Renata combs my hair into place. Vanessa licks her index finger, and it sizzles as she touches the hot iron.

"Ready?" she says.

"Do I really need this?"

"Mia! Ironing your hair is like ironing your clothes. No one likes wrinkles."

Vanessa presses the iron down on my hair and a shot of hot steam scorches my scalp. I scream out in pain and Renata shrieks in sympathy. When I look up at Vanessa, she's smiling her guilty smile.

"Whoops," she says, switching the iron from Steam back to Wool.

Will

When my little brother Dave sees my haircut, he laughs himself stupid.

"What happened, Will? Did you have a fight with a lawn mower?"

"Good one, Dave."

"And the lawn mower won, Will!"

"Looks like it, Dave."

"The lawn mower won, Will! The lawn mower won!"

Dave doesn't mean any harm by it. It's just his crazy sense of humor. Four years ago, when he was nine years old, Dave dived into a swimming pool and hit his head on the bottom. He's a paraplegic now, so he's stuck in a wheelchair for the rest of his life. It's good that he still has a sense of humor. Laughing is probably what keeps him sane.

A lot of people who meet Dave think there must be something wrong with him, more than just his legs, I mean. There were doctors who said the damage to his spine had affected him mentally and others who said his brain was still okay. The way Dave thinks and acts is pretty different from other kids his age. But there's nothing wrong with him. Since his accident, a part of Dave has stayed the same. He's thirteen now, but it's like a part of Dave is still nine years old. When some people meet Dave, they feel really sorry for him, which is pretty stupid. The truth is, Dave is happier than most people I know.

Dave is reading *The Encyclopedia of Tennis* from cover to cover. I don't know how much of it he actually reads, but he certainly enjoys talking about it.

"Will! Will! I'm up to Bjorn Borg! I read Boris Becker and now I'm up to Bjorn Borg! It's got all about him! He was the best, Will! He was better than you!"

"No way, Dave! I could beat Bjorn Borg blindfolded. I could beat him in straight sets: 6–0, 6–0, 6–0."

"You *could not*, Will! You're a liar, Will! Bjorn Borg was the *best*!"

Like me, Dave played a lot of tennis as a kid. I improved only after lots of sweat and working on my technique. Dave was the opposite. He was a natural. He made it look easy. He was the kind of kid who would either serve a double fault or ace you. He had all the talent but none of the discipline. Getting me going about tennis is Dave's substitute for what could have been. Dave might have been a champion, if he'd only had half a chance. After the accident, my dad, Ken, said I would have to train twice as hard. I was playing for both of us now, he said.

Dave's accident hit our family pretty hard. It turned Ken into a personal trainer and fitness fanatic. Lyn—my mom—became Dave's full-time caregiver. She helps Dave with his homework. She helps him in and out of the shower. (Not the toilet, though. Dave is very definite about that.) She gets him dressed in the mornings, then drives him to school in her specially designed car. Lyn is a voluntary worker at Dave's school. She's on the committee and in charge of the fund-raising. She's done lots of workshops and read lots of books about caring for the disabled. She's had handrails and ramps installed throughout our house. She's mapped out each hour of Dave's week. It's her way of dealing with it, I guess.

We never talk about the accident. It's not that we're afraid of talking about it. It's more that we think about going forward instead of backward, if that makes sense. Dave's accident is there for all of us, all the time. It's part of our family, and it's shaped us into who we are. It made us different from other families. Closer, in some ways, and more determined. It's something a normal family wouldn't understand.

"Will! Will! Who's your date for the dance tonight?"

"I haven't got one, Dave."

"Is it the lawn mower, Will? Is that who it is?"

Mia

As expected, Vanessa is a sensation at the dance. In her new stretch jeans and her push-up bra, she has all the boys drooling over her. Like she has bras, Vanessa has a different smile for every occasion. She has a friendly smile, a sympathetic smile, a dumb-girl smile, a teasing smile, a poor-me smile, a crazy smile, an up-yours smile, a flirty smile, and a full-on X-rated smile that always gets her into trouble.

After barely an hour at the dance, Vanessa drags Renata and me back to the bathroom to discuss her latest boy troubles. She takes a swig of gin from the perfume bottle in her shoulder bag. Renata and I both decline.

"There are two boys fighting over me," she says, dabbing at her mascara. "They think they own me."

Renata assures her that competition is a good thing.

"It's natural selection," she says. "Survival of the fittest."

Vanessa is easily consoled. "It's just a school dance," she says. "I'm just flirting."

School dances *can* be a bit of a letdown. You put in the effort to make yourself look nice, then when you get there, you realize you're actually still at school. The band, if there is one, is usually playing its first-ever gig, and the DJ, if there is one, is usually trying to show how cool he is, instead of putting on songs that people actually know. You go along hoping to be swept off your feet by a handsome stranger, but when you get there, you realize there *are* no strangers. Everyone knows everyone else, and no one is taking any chances.

Most of us girls are doing our best under the circumstances, but the boys keep interrupting, trying to drag things back into the gutter. When girls dance, they want to have fun and look good, but when boys dance, they just clown around. Girls close their eyes and dance to the beat, while boys play air guitar. Do they really think we care about that stuff? Do they think acting like that is going to bring girls flocking? I like it when guys are funny, but there's a fine line between funny and goofy. Actually, it's not a fine line. It's more like a bottomless chasm.

Vanessa gets to make out with both boys in the end. Then, while the two of them are outside bashing each other's brains in, Vanessa goes backstage with the DJ to check out his new microphone. Renata and I dance together—boy-free—until they turn on the house lights and tell us all to go home. The boys start bursting balloons and making condom jokes, while the girls try to pretend they can't hear.

As I'm walking out the door, I see Will Holland for the first time that night. He's crouching in the corner with a hat pulled down around his ears. I hardly even recognize him.

Will

According to *The Encyclopedia of Tennis*, you can learn a lot from the way people move. In the chapter called "Biomechanics," there are photographs of famous players, with stick figures to illustrate how they move and the

forces that affect their bodies. To draw "The Kinetic Chain," you divide people's bodies into feet, calves, thighs, back, shoulders, and arms—each element is a straight line, connected by a moving joint.

"To understand the way people move," it says, "you need to understand where their momentum starts from and how it is directed."

The way Mia dances is not referred to in *The Encyclopedia of Tennis*. There is no footnote. It isn't mentioned in the appendix. The way Mia dances is something else. No stick-figure diagram could ever illustrate it. The way Mia dances is like the way she plays her viola. It is something to appreciate, not to analyze. The way Mia dances is just how Mia is. It was there in the way she walked into woodshop and sat down on the stool. It was there in the hallway when she slipped past me and walked away. There is nothing kinetic or biomechanical about it. It's not about momentum or conservation of energy. It isn't something you could ever hope to improve on. No theory would ever understand it. No stick figure could ever describe it.

It's very bendy.

Mia

As I play my viola—*spiccato e maestoso*—I imagine gypsies with bells around their ankles dancing, swallowing swords, eating broken glass, and walking on hot coals. I imagine my bedroom decorated like a gypsy's caravan,

with embroidered cushions and burning incense, hand-woven carpets and tapestries flickering in the candlelight. I imagine an old gypsy woman with a head scarf and golden earrings, holding my palm and telling my fortune.

"Darlink!" she says. "You have a long middle finger. It means you are someone who takes life very seriously. But you have a weak fate line. It means you are unsettled about your future." The gypsy woman studies my fingertips. "You are a daydreamer," she says. "And you have calluses from playing your viola!"

"What about romance?" I ask. "Do you see any romance?"

The old woman shakes her head. "Your heart line is straight. It means you are waiting for something or someone. But look, darlink! The Apollo line, the line of the sun. It means you will be happy, in the end."

Will

On the oval at lunchtime there are boys who line up to wrestle each other with one hand behind their backs. If you lose, you go to the back of the line. If you win, you get to be champion and take on the next guy. As an alternative to this line-wrestling game, one kid has set up a chess-board, so that others can line up to play him at chess. His name is Kevin Hunt, but everyone calls him Yorick (as in "Alas, poor Yorick"). Yorick is a "gifted learner." He is famous as the school math champion, but also as the kid who threw up during the Life Education talks.

The Monday after the school dance, I sit myself down at Yorick's chessboard. I don't know why, exactly. I've played chess before, but I'm certainly not expecting to win. At least I know Yorick won't notice my near-fatal haircut.

Yorick hides a pawn in each hand, and I choose the black.

"White moves first," says Yorick, with a painful smile.

Yorick and I set up our pieces and start playing. With every move he makes, Yorick announces the position: "Pawn to queen four" . . . "Knight to king's bishop three." He is fast, but not totally out of my league. Gradually, I start taking longer with my moves, and Yorick begins to lose interest. But I am hanging in there. I haven't made a fool of myself yet. It is one of those tight games where no one wants to sacrifice any pieces. I am giving it 100 percent of my concentration, while Yorick picks at his fingernails and talks about mathematical theories.

"Topology," he explains, "is about the connections *between* things, rather than their shape or size. It's about the things that remain unchanged, even after an object is bent, broken, or twisted . . . Queen to bishop six."

I scratch my head and try to concentrate on the chess game. Yorick isn't trying to distract me or even impress me. He's just desperate to tell someone.

"Theoretical geometry . . ." He sighs. "The possibilities are endless."

Slowly, with each move, the chess game becomes more complex. I have long ago lost the thread of what Yorick is saying, but it hasn't dampened his enthusiasm.

I am beginning to make a few silly moves now. I have lost a few valuable pieces. When I look up from the chessboard and see Mia Foley walk past—topology or no topology—I know I'm toast.

"What can I do?" I ask Yorick. "It's hopeless."

Yorick surveys my pieces and sadly shakes his head.

"When you have very few options," he replies, "you need a bold, almost suicidal move that throws the game open."

After thinking about this, I pick up my knight and brilliantly capture his queen.

Two moves later, Yorick has me in checkmate.

Mia

The next day, at lunchtime, there's a note on my locker:

Q. What's the difference between a viola and a lawn mower?

A. You can tune a lawn mower.

—W.

I read Will's note, then screw it up into a ball and throw it away. Renata sees the crumpled paper lying there, but before she can get to it, I dive on the note and stuff it in my bra.

"You should use cotton wool." Vanessa smiles. "It's softer."

"It's a viola joke," I explain. "Not very funny, either."

"Ah!" says Renata. "From a secret admirer?"

"It's the Tracksuit, isn't it?" says Vanessa.

I nod.

"Is he giving you a hard time?" says Vanessa. "Watch this. I'll fix him."

"No! No! I didn't mean—"

But it's too late. Vanessa hitches up her dress, flicks back her hair, then goes off in search of Will. Renata follows, dragging me with her. Out on the oval, we see Vanessa towering over Will with her long, suntanned legs. I almost can't bear to watch.

Vanessa sits down beside Will, and they talk for a while. Then Vanessa stands up suddenly and storms back to us.

"That guy," she announces, "is *so* gay!"

Will

I am sitting there, minding my own business, when Vanessa Webb—the superbabe, the wildest and most experienced girl in the whole school, the girl who reduces even the toughest guys to babbling idiots—walks up to me, smiling.

"Will?" she says, with a tilt of her head.

"Vanessa?"

"Can I sit down?"

Vanessa Webb sits down next to me, and I feel her bare knee brush against my leg. Her face is very close now. All of her is very close. She is still smiling, but now her smile has a teasing, dangerous look about it. I know it's a trap. I know I'm being set up.

Vanessa Webb takes a deep breath and tucks her hair behind one ear. Everything about her body is asking me to look at her, but I know looking anywhere except her face would be a mistake. My first impulse is to move away, but I stay where I am, trying hard to hold her seductive gaze. If I had read *Cosmo Girl!* magazine, I wonder, would I know how to deal with the situation?

"Will, are you Mia's secret admirer?"

"Umm . . ."

"Will," she whispers, "can you be my secret admirer, too?"

In Dealing with Dangerous Women, our experts suggest the following options:

1. *Fight fire with fire—assume Vanessa is flirting and flirt back.*
2. *Let the fire run its course—sit there under a blanket until Vanessa sees how ridiculous she is being.*
3. *Throw a bucket of water on the fire—do a loud fart or pick your nose.*
4. *Panic!—break the glass and call the fire department.*

"You don't need to do this," I say.

Vanessa frowns. "Do what?"

"You try too hard, Vanessa. You're nicer-looking than you think you are."

I don't know why I say it, or even if it makes any sense. But for one brief moment, Vanessa hesitates. I can see a flash of doubt in her eyes. It's just a flash, then the doubt is gone and Vanessa is looking at me as if I'm a rotting carcass and she is a gourmet vegetarian.

"What the hell are you talking about?" she demands.

Before I can answer, she stands up and storms off.

Mia

Vanessa had been with her latest boyfriend for about ten minutes when she decided that she, Renata, and I should go out with the guy and his two best friends. We go to the movies together—the three of us girls and these three big workout kings with flat heads and no necks. We sit in the back row, according to where Vanessa tells us. When she and her new boy start making out, Renata and I are expected to do likewise. The movie has only just started when I feel my date's arm land heavily across my shoulder. I feel like that woman from *Gorillas in the Mist*. I shrug off King Kong and try to concentrate on the movie, but five minutes later, I feel his hairy fingers crawling toward my boobs! Instead of slapping him across the face, I lean forward and offer him a breath mint: *It's moments like these.*

Luckily, it's an Arnold Schwarzenegger movie, and the action is starting to pick up. Picking bits of mint from his teeth and laughing loudly, Kong soon forgets all about me. I look across at Vanessa with her hand inside her guy's pocket, then at Renata, doing her best to keep her legs crossed. No amount of breath mints will save them now.

Vanessa has been on the pill since she was fourteen. The way she talks to Renata and me about it, you'd think being a virgin was a punishable offense. Vanessa talks big, but

secretly I wonder if she really does jump into bed with the guys she meets. She is always comparing guys and saying how few of them "measure up." But I don't know if Vanessa actually *does it* with as many guys as she says she does. The truth is, she had the pill prescribed for her period pain.

After the movie, we are sitting around eating ice cream while the Arnie clones reenact the entire movie for us. On the far side of the food court Vanessa spots Will pushing a kid in a wheelchair.

"Look!" she says. "Will Holland is a male nurse. That *proves* he's gay!"

Arnie A thinks this is hilarious. "Homos helping the handicapped!" he roars.

"It won't be long," says Arnie B, "before they give queers their own parking places, too."

"Imagine the signs," snorts Arnie C. "They'd be pink, wouldn't they?"

"Boys are like parking places," says Vanessa. "All the good ones are taken, and only the disabled are left."

Everyone laughs except Arnie A. "Are you calling me a crip?" he says.

"Don't call them that," I say. "It could happen to you one day."

No one says a word. Vanessa looks embarrassed, but Arnie A just smiles. When he speaks, his voice is softer, and his eyes have started glazing over.

"If it *did* happen," he says, "I wouldn't just sit around like a *crip*, feeling sorry for myself. I'd work out, day and night,

till I could walk again. There's nothing you can't overcome if you try. It's all about willpower and never giving up."

Stupid people say stupid things, so I don't know why it upsets me so much. According to Arnie A, if you were disabled, it must be your fault somehow.

"You're only saying that," I tell him, "because you don't want to think about how it would feel, being stuck in a wheelchair for the rest of your life."

Will

Dave and I go to SportsWorld and buy two pairs of Adidas tennis shoes. Dave always says he's going to buy something different, but when he sees the shoes on me, he changes his mind and insists on a pair of the same. You might think it's weird, spending a hundred bucks on shoes for a kid who can't walk, but I think it's brilliant. For starters, they'll never wear out.

Decked out in our new shoes, Dave and I go to the food court for a doughnut. With all those stunning girls walking past us, it isn't long before Dave is whispering to me across the table.

"Have you got a girlfriend, Will?"

"No, Dave. Have you?"

"Will! I'm being serious!"

"There's this girl at school," I say, trying to sound casual. Dave is shocked. "Do you *like* her, Will?"

"I don't know, Dave. I don't know what to do next."

Dave is impressed. "You could take her horseback riding, Will."

"I can't take her horseback riding, Dave."

"Sure you can, Will! Girls love horses!"

"This girl is different, Dave. She likes ... Actually, I don't know what she likes."

"Then maybe she *does* like horses! All girls love horses, Will!"

"Dave! I am *not* taking her horseback riding, okay?"

"Ponies?"

"Not horses or ponies or camels or llamas!"

"Don't be stupid, Will! Now you're just being stupid."

"I'm not sure about this girl, Dave. I'm not sure if she even likes me."

Dave shakes his head and looks at his new shoes.

"You could ask her to the tennis match, Will."

"The tennis match? No way!"

Mia

I am in the library, looking for a book about beagles. I want to know when Harriet will stop being such a baby. When will she be an adult? Will she be a teenage dog first? Will Harriet get pimples and start acting like I don't own her anymore?

Through a gap in the bookshelf I see Will Holland in the next aisle. I look away before he sees me, but then something pulls me back. Instead, I take down a book to make

the gap bigger.

"What's the difference between a viola and a lawn mower?" I whisper.

Will spins around, startled, but when he sees my face in among the books, he laughs. "One makes an awful noise?"

"And the other is used for cutting grass."

One by one, Will and I remove more books so we can talk face-to-face.

"How's Vanessa?" he grins. "Is she still mad at me?"

"She thinks you're a chess nerd with a bad haircut."

"Is that all?"

"She also called you a gay nurse in a smelly tracksuit."

"Nurse?"

"We saw you, yesterday, at the shopping center. You were pushing a kid in a wheelchair."

Will nods. "That's Dave."

"It made me think, you know. I mean, it must be good to have a job like that. Just to be doing something useful."

"It's not a job. Dave's my brother."

"Oh . . . I'm sorry."

"Don't feel bad about it. Dave will love it when I tell him. He's always wishing he had a nurse to order around. He's got friends at his school who have their own nurses. It's a status thing, like having a butler or a chauffeur."

"Can't he come to our school?"

"His reading and writing are good enough. It's just . . . there are too many steps."

"That's not fair."

Will shrugs. "Violins Rule."

"So," I say. "A secret for a secret. Except I don't suppose your brother is a secret. I just wanted to say thanks, for not telling anyone about my dad."

"Who would I tell?"

"I'm pretty sure it's nothing, by the way. My dad wouldn't do something like that."

Will nods diplomatically. "So are we officially talking again?"

"We were never officially *not* talking."

"We were never officially anything," he says.

Will

Ken is not happy. "Keep your head still and both feet on the ground," he says. "Rotate your upper body. Throw to the peak of your reach and strike when the ball reaches the apex. Remember, a low toss gives you more time to hit the ball, not less."

Ken is my dad. He's also my coach.

Ken says I am throwing the ball too high. The higher you throw the ball, he says, the faster it comes down, so the harder it is to hit. It sounds good in theory. But in practice, old habits die hard.

Ken shows me how to do it several times, using different ways of holding the ball. I copy him with every throw, and we do it over and over until the ball reaches the right

height. We try it with my throwing hand to the side, cupping the ball with the fingers. We try it with my throwing hand down, holding the ball gently between the fingertips. In the end we go back to the way I've always done it—the way most people do it—with the ball balanced in the open upward palm. Now I am throwing the ball to the right height, but I can't hit it properly. I feel cramped and off balance. I am serving the ball short, without speed or accuracy. And Ken is not happy.

Ken is from the old school, the McEnroe-Connors-Lendl era of the huge serve and power game. Ken thinks I am serving like a ballerina.

"Okay," he says. "Let's try the towel trick."

Ken gets a plain white towel and wraps it around my head, covering my face so I can't see. Dave thinks this is hysterical.

"You look like a mummy, Will!" he laughs.

Ken's theory is that throwing the ball should be automatic.

"Watching the ball only confuses you," he says. "To throw the ball to the height of the outstretched racket, you shouldn't have to think about it."

I am starting to think Ken has seen too many *Star Wars* movies: *Use the Force, Will*. . . .

The towel feels heavy and lopsided on my head. I can't see a thing, and the muffled hearing is upsetting my balance. After six complete misses, Dave is crying with laughter.

Ken, on the other hand, has gone into Darth Vader mode.

"Concentrate!" he says, sternly.

"I thought the idea was *not* to concentrate."

This time, when I throw the ball, it comes down and hits me on the head. Dave goes into hysterics and almost falls out of his wheelchair. I've had enough.

I tear off the towel and throw it onto the ground.

"I can't do it. It's a stupid idea anyway."

"I wanna do it!" shouts Dave. "Please, Ken! Let me do the towel trick!"

Ken is staring hard at the ground—definitely not happy.

"Go on," I say. "Give him a go."

"Come on, Ken! Give me a go!"

Ken looks at me and shakes his head. "You donkey!"

According to *The Encyclopedia of Tennis*, "donkey" is an old-fashioned word for "loser."

Together, Ken and I tie the towel around Dave's head. We watch as he throws up the ball, then grips the rim to steady his wheelchair as he brings down the racket. Blindfolded, he hits the ball cleanly over the net and into the middle of the service square.

"See!" Dave laughs. "You should be coaching *me*, Ken!"

Mia

Strained smiles and whispered conversations. Harriet barking endlessly because she hasn't been walked. Empty wine bottles with only one glass. Takeout food, again. Dad working late, again. Mom watching junk TV.

"Are you okay, Mom?"

"I'm fine, darling."

"You don't look fine."

"I'm just tired, that's all."

I can't talk to my mom about it. I'm not sure there's anything to talk about, anyway. I'm not 100 percent sure she even knows what's happening.

When Dad gets home, they argue about petty things. Easy things, like a piece of furniture or a painting on the wall.

"You said you liked it," she says.

"I said I could live with it," he says.

"Isn't that the same thing?" she says.

"No," he says. "In fact, it's the opposite."

I go to my room to practice *The Four Seasons: Winter*. It's cold and bleak—*frigado e eremo*—and my head is numb with unanswered questions: Did my parents ever love each other? Why did they get married? Is it possible to love someone, if they don't love you? Is love like the chicken or the egg? Or is it just a burned chicken omelette?

I wish I was as deaf as Beethoven, so I didn't have to hear them fighting. I wish my bedroom was a flotation tank with soundproofed walls. I could float in absolute darkness, hearing nothing. Seeing nothing, smelling, tasting, and feeling nothing . . .

Will

Dear Mia,

Q. What's the difference between a viola and a lawn mower?

A. A lawn mower sounds better in a string quartet.

It was good talking to you the other day. That's the problem with us going to the same school—it's hard to talk without feeling like you're on "Candid Camera."

Are you busy this Saturday? If not, here is a free ticket to the tennis tournament (at the big stadium in the city, do you know it?). It's short notice, and I know you don't even like tennis, but if you want to come that would be great. (Don't worry if you don't because my dad got the ticket for free.) We could have lunch there. (I'll pay!)

Let me know if you can make it.

—W.

Mia

When I see Will at school the next day I thank him for the ticket and say I'll try to make it, but we both know there isn't much chance. I'm not sure if I'm ready to go out on a date with Will yet. And when I am ready, I think it should be something we both want to do. Something more memorable than going to watch tennis. And, anyway, it *is* short notice.

I wimp out, in other words.

When I wake up on Saturday morning, Mom and Dad are at the breakfast table. Dad is reading the *Financial Review* and Mom is reading *Vogue*.

I say, "Good morning."

My father smiles and says something about health insurance.

My mother smiles and says something about getting the chairs reupholstered.

When I open the back door, Harriet jumps all over me. Outside, it's a beautiful day, but inside the thermometer reads cold and icy. I have to get out of the house. I'm sure there are plenty of girls who get the urge to run away, but the thing that holds them back is having nowhere to go.

I look at the clock and think about Will's ticket, pinned to my noticeboard. The tennis I can take or leave, but at least there will be blue skies and sunshine. And Will is a blue-sky expert.

I take a quick shower and throw on some clothes.

"Where are you going, darling?"

"Out."

"What about Harriet? Can't you take her with you?"

"Harriet is a *dog*, Mom."

Sweet revenge! Without looking back, I shut the front door and head off to the bus stop. As soon as I'm out of the house, my mood changes completely. No wonder tennis is such a popular sport! No wonder everyone wears Nike!

My bus is late, so I miss the connection with my train and have to wait half an hour for the next one. There are clouds in the sky now, and the day is not as summery as the dress I've chosen. What's worse, in my hurry to leave,

I've forgotten my glasses. There is no point turning back, though. What revenge would there be in that?

My train finally comes and I sit down opposite two boys who spend the whole trip trying to impress me with stories of their ex-girlfriends. (Boys just do not get it, do they?) It's not long before I am staring out the window, thinking about viola jokes, and hoping Will will be pleased to see me.

In the city, trying to make up for lost time, I run for a bus and snap a heel. I twist my ankle, and it hurts so much I want to cry. I wait for the next bus to the stadium, then I limp across to the St. John's Ambulance guys to check that I haven't broken anything. The heel is unfixable, and those shoes weren't cheap. By the time they have bandaged my ankle, it's after twelve, and I'm sure Will thinks I'm not coming. I hobble up to the gate to present my ticket, but the lady sadly shakes her head.

"I'm sorry, madam, but this is the center court. Your ticket is for court number two."

"But I'm supposed to be meeting someone. There must be some mistake."

"I'm sorry, madam. All the seats are taken."

Court number two is half empty. I'm shown to my seat, and guess what?

No Will.

Even without my glasses, I can see that the game on court two is pretty ordinary. Most of the people watching are eating lunch or chatting.

I wait for half an hour, but Will never shows. The tennis

match finishes, and the players shake hands across the net. I am cold and hungry, and my ankle is painfully swollen. Too miserable for words, I get up and catch a taxi home. I swear, tennis is *such* a stupid sport. I don't know what people see in it.

Will

It takes a lot of nerve to call a girl. You can't just sit down and dial the number. You have to be prepared—physically, mentally, and emotionally. You have to be relaxed, but alert. You have to make like it's no big deal, but you can't be too offhand, either. If she wants to talk about bank profits and Third World debt, you might suddenly be in over your head. Calling any girl is tricky enough, but calling *the* girl is like taking a bathysphere to the bottom of the ocean.

To call a girl, what you need more than anything is privacy. The phone must be in a separate room, away from your family—preferably your own bedroom, and preferably at the far end of the house. To achieve this you need a long telephone extension cord. The door to the room must be solid enough to prevent eavesdropping and/or forced entry. Ideally, it should be lockable, but a suitable barricade like a heavy chair or desk will do. The windows should be shut and the curtains drawn. Lighting should be subtle and unobtrusive. All electrical appliances—radios, computers, alarm clocks, etc.—should be switched off. Even the faintest noise can be a distraction.

I unwrap my fifty-foot extension cord and plug it into the telephone socket. I unravel it down the hall, under my bedroom door and into the closet, just to be on the safe side. Feeling nervous and terribly unprepared, I practice dialing the number with the receiver down. I clear my throat, take a deep breath, then dial again—this time for real.

The phone rings once, twice, three times. I am just about to hang up when Mia answers.

"Hello?"

"What's the difference between a viola and a lawn mower?"

"A viola never lets you down."

"I can explain."

"Where *were* you?"

"I was there."

"No, you weren't."

"I saw you. I waved, but you didn't see me."

"Where *were* you?"

"Are you okay? I saw you limping."

"I hurt my ankle."

"I'm really sorry. Is it too late? Can I come over and explain?"

"What? Here? To my house? Now?"

I hear the sound of voices through the muffled receiver, then Mia's mother comes on the phone.

"Mia needs to rest," she says. "She's had enough disappointment for one day."

Then she hangs up.

When I try calling back, the phone is off the hook.

I emerge from my bedroom closet a nervous wreck. I can't wait until Monday. By Monday Mia will have told her friends, and the whole school will be convinced that I am a creep.

According to *The Encyclopedia of Tennis*, a "scrambler" is a player who manages to get the ball back somehow, though not very stylishly.

I have to visit her. I've got no choice.

It is after nine by the time I get to Mia's house—not the ideal time to visit. It doesn't look like the kind of house where people drop in uninvited, especially not nervous guys who have been told to stay away. There is a light on at the back of the house, but not the kind of light that makes you feel welcome. It's the kind of light you have on when you've had enough disappointments for one day and you want to be left alone.

But I have no choice. I have to clear things up.

I walk up to the front door. The doorbell light glows orange as my finger hovers above it. I start rehearsing my apology: *Mrs. Foley, I'm sorry to disturb you. I know it's late* . . . From inside the house I hear footsteps coming down the hall. And I haven't even rung the doorbell yet! In shock, I turn and run out the gate. I'm halfway down the street before I stop and look back. I need a better plan. I need to avoid Mia's mother at all costs.

I consider leaving a note in the mailbox, but I don't have a pen or paper on me. I consider phoning the fire department and reporting that a neighbor's house is burning, but having all the street come out to watch is no guarantee that Mia and I will get to talk. I have no other options. It is time to do the scariest and most clichéd of all the Hollywood love scenes. I will have to serenade Mia outside her bedroom window.

I climb the gate and sneak down the side of the house. When a dog suddenly starts barking, I freeze with dread. Mia never mentioned having a lovable pit bull, or a rottweiler who secretly dismembers visiting tradesmen and buries their bones in the garden. Barking madly, the dog comes bounding toward me out of the darkness. There is nowhere to hide, so I jump into the garden, trampling a bed of daffodils. As I try to run, the dog leaps up at me, barking loud enough to wake the whole street. I fall to my knees, but instead of ripping my throat out, the dog paws and licks me. It's not a rottweiler, it's a beagle! I wrestle her to the ground, then smack her bottom hard so that she yelps and runs away.

There are two windows on this side of the house, but only one with a light on. Through a crack in the curtain I can see Mia sitting on her bed, dressing her swollen ankle. Her ankle isn't the only part of Mia that needs dressing. She is only wearing panties and a T-shirt. Her ankle looks pretty bad, but the rest of her looks pretty good. I am mesmerized. I can't look away. I've been granted the first of three wishes and if I wait, Mia will soon move on to wish number two. Then I realize what I am doing. I have come to serenade Mia, but I have ended up as a Peeping Tom outside her window!

But how do I serenade her? I don't even know what the word means.

Using a loose definition—i.e., to "serenade" means "to get her attention"—I start tapping on the window as lightly as I can. I try tapping more like a friend than an ax-wielding maniac, but all tapping on windows sounds pretty much the same, in the middle of the night. And when Mia hears it, she dives off the bed and switches off the light.

"Who's that?" she whispers.

"It's me, Will! Open the window."

"What are you doing here?"

"I had to see you, to explain about today. How's your ankle?"

"*Go away!*"

Suddenly, there is a knock on her bedroom door.

"Are you all right, darling? Did you want something?" says her mom.

Mia closes the curtains and jumps back into bed as the door opens.

"I . . . just called out good night, that's all."

"Good night, dear."

"Good night, Mom."

When Mrs. Foley is gone, Mia opens the window. She is wearing her bathrobe now. Her face is so close, I could reach out and touch it.

"I won't stay long, I promise."

"I don't care what excuse you've got. I don't want to hear it. This is not a love scene, okay? This is not Romeo and Juliet, and you are *not* Leonardo DiCaprio. I'm sure you're sorry. I'm sure you've got a good excuse. But that doesn't mean I want to elope with you, okay?"

"I'm sorry about today. I was there. In fact, I waved at you. If you'd worn your glasses, you would have seen me."

"I don't need my glasses to see someone sitting next to me," Mia hissed.

"I was on the court. I was right in front of you."

"What? Were you chasing tennis balls?"

"Kind of . . . I was—"

"Look, I've had a miserable day. I don't know why you invited me to the tennis match—I hate tennis! I don't know why I bothered. . . . All I want to do now is forget it. So could you *please* leave me alone!"

Before I get another chance to speak, Mia closes her window and draws her curtains. The last thing I hear is the sound of her falling onto her bed.

three

Mia

On Monday morning we have assembly outside in the courtyard. All the students are lined up—seventh-graders at the front and twelfth-graders at the back—that is, everyone except me. Because of my swollen ankle, I am allowed to sit with my foot up, watching from the side. Being on crutches is a real pain, but it does have some advantages.

We sing the national anthem. Next there are the usual news items from various teachers, then the principal steps up to make an important announcement.

"I would like to congratulate one of our students on a marvelous achievement. Over the weekend he played at the State Tennis Center and won the Under Sixteen Championship. Congratulations, Will Holland!"

Everyone claps as Will makes his way to the front. Kids are patting him on the back, and teachers are shaking his hand. With a crutch under one arm, I ease myself up for a better view. As Will shakes the principal's hand, I reach for my second crutch, lose my balance, and fall to the ground. I lie there in a heap, helpless and invisible, as the principal presents Will with his trophy.

"On behalf of the school," she says, "I'd like to say, Well done, Will, and best of luck for the future!"

When I look up at the sky, I expect it to rain down tennis balls.

Will

The gym teacher wants to know all the details, the teacher on lunch duty asks how to improve her backhand, the basketballers want me to make up a team, and the arm wrestlers invite me to stand at the head of the line. Even Yorick gives me an approving nod.

Thank you for calling Superstars Incorporated. Please hold the line while we transfer you to another universe. . . .

When the seventh-grade girls come and ask for my autograph, I'm sure they must be joking. One of them gives me a felt-tipped pen but no paper to write on. Instead, she holds out her arm, so I sign it *Will Holl*—, doing it fast and messy like a celebrity. The next girl turns up the hem of her dress, and a third rolls down her sock.

"It tickles!" She laughs as I initial her ankle: *W. H.*

The last seventh-grade girl wants me to sign her underwear, but I refuse.

"It would look pretty ridiculous," I say. "You bending over while I write my name on your butt."

"I could take them off," she suggests.

Before I have time to object, she takes off her panties and holds them out.

According to *The Encyclopedia of Tennis*, a "sitter" is an easy opportunity—a softly hit ball, close to the net and well within reach.

"Sorry," I say. "I don't do underpants."

Mia

"Oh, my God!" screams Vanessa.

"Oh, my God!" squeals Renata.

"I don't believe it," gasps Vanessa. "He's got groupies!"

"He's signing their clothes!" Renata screeches.

"He's signing their bodies!" Vanessa shrieks.

"They love it!" giggles Renata.

"*He* loves it!" sniggers Vanessa.

"It's tragic," I say.

"Pathetic," says Renata.

"Boys are like that," says Vanessa. "They love being chased by younger girls."

"My father's like that," I suddenly blurt out. "He's got a girlfriend half his age!"

"Your father?" says Renata.

"Since when?" says Vanessa.

"It's truly disgusting," I say. "He thinks it's a secret. He thinks Mom doesn't know."

"Oh, Mia!" says Renata. "You poor thing!"

"My dad's the same," says Vanessa. "He goes to those men's clubs in the city, where the girls dance on the tables."

"Have you seen those girls!" says Renata. "Have you seen the G-strings they wear!"

"Imagine the bikini wax!" says Vanessa.

"Some of them wax *all over*," says Renata.

"I *know*!" says Vanessa.

One moment I'm sharing my deepest, darkest secret

with my two best friends. Next moment it feels as if I'm in a hair salon, discussing body wax and gossiping about tabletop dancers.

Will

When I tell Dave about the seventh-grade girls, he gets *that look* on his face again.

"What about me, Will? I'm in the seventh grade! Did you tell them about me?"

"I said you were already taken, Dave. Engaged to Anna Kournikova."

Dave laughs loudly. "You did not, Will!"

"But Anna wants to break it off. She's heard about you and Venus Williams."

Dave shakes his head. "You *did not* say that, Will!"

"Venus *and* Serena!"

"Tell the truth, Will!"

"*And* Pat Rafter. It was mixed doubles, I told them."

"Stop it, Will! Not with Pat Rafter, okay?"

"Why not, Dave? He's good-looking, isn't he?"

"Will! Pat Rafter's a boy! And I'm not *like that*, okay?"

"Sorry, Dave. I was just kidding."

"Then say it. Dave Holland is not gay. Go on. Say it, Will."

"Dave Holland is not gay."

"And neither is Pat Rafter."

"And neither is Pat Rafter."

I like teasing Dave. That's what big brothers do. It's part

of our job description. But I also do it to stop the conversation taking a predictable nose-dive. When Dave starts talking about sex, it's hard to stop him.

"Dave Holland's dick still works. Go on, Will . . . Say it."

"Dave Holland's dick still works."

"He's a good kisser."

"He's a good kisser."

"He does it with all the girls."

"He does it with all the boys."

"Will!"

"Sorry, Dave."

Mia

Vanessa's latest boy craze is the St. D**** boys. Most days, after school, we hang around with the St. D. boys up at the shops. They don't have girls at their school, so they buy us milkshakes and fries and let Vanessa bum their smokes. I don't have a problem with smoking. If someone offers me a cigarette, I'll take it if I have to. But inhaling makes me cough, so I've learned how to look like I'm smoking without actually doing it.

The St. D. boys are okay. They're pretty harmless. They throw their schoolbags onto the road in front of oncoming cars. They jump off walls and risk their lives, just to get our attention. They say, "I'm the best!" and they call each other "Fag," "Prick," or "Useless." But when they talk to us girls, they say "Peter," "John," or "Michael"—I don't get it. As far as I can see, the most interesting thing about them is that they're from another school. I swear Vanessa only raves about them to make the boys at our school jealous.

We are outside the deli, watching the St. D. boys perform on their skateboards, when I see Will and Yorick coming. They are walking along the sidewalk, deep in conversation, when one of the boys falls off his skateboard and goes tumbling into them. Yorick drops his schoolbag, and chess pieces go everywhere. The guy gets up and brushes himself off without an apology. But then Will grabs his skateboard and holds it behind his back.

"Better help him pick them up, don't you think?" says Will.

The guy looks at the spilled chessmen, then over at his friends.

"You knocked into me," says Yorick, getting down on his knees. "You should help me pick them up!"

The guy looks at Yorick and laughs. Instantly, two of his friends ride over and start circling them. Will and Yorick are surrounded, but instead of looking scared, Will is completely cool. He's either being very stupid or very brave.

I am dreading what will happen next, when Vanessa calls out to them.

"Hey, guys! Don't you know who this is? It's Will Holland, the famous tennis star!"

Will looks surprised. The boys keep circling. Finally Vanessa has a chance to get even with the one boy who's ever rejected her.

"For your information," she says, "Will is a legend at our school. If you want him to sign that skateboard, you should give him a pen. Otherwise, just be good boys and do what he says."

With the chessmen safely back in their box, Yorick is satisfied, and Will gives back the skateboard. The other boys make a gap for the two of them to come over.

"Are they always that obedient?" Will asks.

Vanessa smiles. "They've been well trained."

"Cyborgs!" Yorick laughs. "Replicants!"

Vanessa's smile is hard to pick. It's not her typical boy-smile by any means—not from her supervixen repertoire, at least. Vanessa's smile is simple and matter-of-fact. It's sweet, like the girl next door. Vanessa is flirting with Will, by not flirting!

Will looks at me, meaningfully. "If you make a mess, you should clean it up."

I look away. With Vanessa and Renata there, I don't know what to say.

"Poor Mia," Vanessa shakes her head. "She looks like Long John Silver with those crutches. She should walk around with a parrot on her shoulder. *Arh! Shiver me timbers!*"

Vanessa does the pirate voice, and Will plays the parrot.

"Polly want a cracker?"

Renata looks puzzled. Yorick looks lost. Then Vanessa does the parrot voice and Will falls down laughing. "Polly want a Ritz Bitz?" "Polly want a Wheat Thin?"

If it doesn't sound very funny, that's because it isn't!

I pick up my schoolbag and limp off up the street. When I look back, Vanessa and Will are still at it, imitating each other like two stupid parrots, laughing uncontrollably.

Will

To relax after training, Dave and I go to the pool. Ken and Lyn thought Dave would never swim again after his accident. He knew how to swim before the accident, but for almost a year after he wouldn't go anywhere near water. Even having a bath would upset him. But then slowly Dave learned to confront his fears. He started off in the baby pool, then graduated to a life jacket. Now Dave loves swimming. He'd swim every day if you let him.

Dave gets into the pool unassisted. He grabs hold of the handrails, pulls himself up out of his wheelchair, steadies, then lowers himself into the water and starts swimming.

"Hey, Will! Look at me! I'm a dolphin!"

With his head up out of the water, his arms splashing wildly and legs trailing limply behind, Dave swims lap after lap without stopping. Dave could swim for hours—he's amazingly fit and strong in his upper body. Getting him out of the water, though, can be almost impossible.

"I don't want to, Will! Just five more minutes! Ten more, at least!"

"But there are chips, Dave. Remember?"

Afterward we sit in the café and watch while Dave studies the vending machine, reading out loud while he tries to make up his mind. "A1: Plain chips . . . A2: Sour cream and onion . . . A3: Salt and vinegar . . . A4: Texas Barbecue . . . Hey, Will! Are those too spicy for me?" Dave considers his options carefully before choosing his trademark packet of onion rings instead.

"Would you go on TV, Will? Would you talk to Oprah Winfrey?"

"Only if I'm really famous, Dave."

"Would you move away from home, Will? Would you have your own swimming pool?"

"I'd live by the beach, Dave. In the Caribbean."

"You're not going to live in a caravan, are you, Will?"

"Car-ib-be-an, Dave. We can sit around all day, drinking pineapple juice."

"Can I come to the Caribbean, Will? Except I don't like pineapple juice. Would there be other types of juice, Will, in the Caribbean?"

"Any juice you want, Dave."

"Will there be chips, Will?"

"Chips *and* onion rings, Dave."

"But there won't be drugs, Will?"

"No drugs, Dave. And no seventh-grade girls, either."

Mia

At morning recess, Renata makes her big announcement.

"Guess what!" she says. "I am going to Europe!"

Renata starts talking about Europe, as if America is

somehow kitsch now. She uses the words "exquisite" and "sophisticated." She talks about the exchange rate and the Eurodollar. Her family is going back to Yugoslavia, now that the political situation has changed. She is going "home" to see "her country." For years, Renata has not been able to mention the Y-word, and now she won't stop talking about it.

"In Yugoslavia," she says, "it's safe to meet your friends in cafés at night."

By the end of recess, Vanessa and I have had enough. It's stupid, but I feel betrayed—as if Renata is going away at a time when I really need her.

"Who does she think she is?" I say, while Renata goes off to get a drink.

"She's such a user!" says Vanessa. "They come here to make money, then they go back home to spend it."

Badmouthing Renata to her face is okay—Renata is always putting herself down—but doing it behind her back is different.

"Don't say that!" I snap. "This is Renata's home, as much as ours."

For a moment, Vanessa almost looks hurt. Then her face changes.

"You are *so* boring, Mia," she says. "No wonder you can't get a boyfriend!"

Will

To-do list:

1. *Design Web page, including a short biography, fan club details, and advice for young players. What inspires you? What do you eat? How do you maintain fitness? Hobbies? Interests? Who would you most like to meet?*

2. ~~*Phone Mia*~~

   Approach publishers re autobiography: Will Holland— Tennis Ace.

   (May need a ghostwriter to do this.)

3. ~~*Send Mia some flowers*~~

   Approach corporate sponsors, i.e., Adidas, Nike, etc. No tobacco companies! (May need an agent to do this.)

4. ~~*No more viola jokes!*~~

   Photo for Web page? (May need new roll of film.)

5. *Begin legal proceedings against Ricki the barber.*

Mia

It's official. Vanessa and I are fighting. Vanessa *was* my best friend, but now she is my enemy for all eternity.

The next day, to avoid Vanessa at recess, I sit on the grass in the place where Will used to sit, before the seventh-grade girls came and offered their bodies on a plate. Sports stars are notoriously sleazy, but I couldn't have imagined Will messing around with girls who aren't even size 34A yet! I thought Will Holland was different from other boys. I thought he was inspired by soaring eagles. I thought his heart was as clear as the clear blue sky, but I was wrong. . . . When I lie back and look up at the sky, the clouds all look like clouds to me. It's even a challenge trying to make them look like woolly sheep.

Am I really boring?

At lunchtime, in orchestra practice, we work on our bowing. It's not enough just to know all the notes and when to play them. They have to be played the right way with the right tone, which means all the viola players bowing up and down at the same time. Ms. S. shows the first viola how to play the passage, then the first viola explains to the rest of us how to mark the score. A lot of our time in rehearsal is spent marking the sheet music with little hats and arrows. It's an important part of playing music, but it can be pretty dull.

Maybe Vanessa is right. Maybe my whole life is boring.

I remember back to that day Will came to watch us—how he made us all laugh, then returned to take a bow. Maybe, just for fun, I should buy Will a conductor's baton for his birthday. I will have to find out when his birthday is. Knowing Will's birthday will tell me what his star sign is, and whether we are compatible, not that I really believe in astrology. Does Will believe in astrology, I wonder? Is he much older than me? Would it matter if I was older than him? Maybe Will is an earth sign—practical and good at tennis. Or maybe he is an air sign—always looking up at the sky. Would certain zodiac signs be better at kissing, I wonder? Would others expect to have their toes sucked?

I hear Ms. S.'s fingernails drumming impatiently on the back of my chair.

"Mia Foley!" she says. "What on earth are you day-dreaming about?"

Will

When Dave comes to watch me train, he sits on the net and does the line calls. He yells them loudly, the way people do in the tournaments: "Let!" "Fault!" "Out!" The calls come fast and clear, and they're always right. You'd never want to argue a line call with Dave. He'd run you down!

Usually, Dave and I hit the ball around together after training. Sometimes we even play a set. Dave is surprisingly fast around the court, and he can hit these mighty ground shots—hard and deep. Dave plays on the baseline, a lot like Bjorn Borg—he never comes up to the net. According to the rules of wheelchair tennis, he's allowed two bounces, and I'm allowed one. Dave wants to win, of course, but he doesn't want charity. He's deadly serious, and he never shows any sign of how he's feeling. The Ice Borg on Wheels, I call him.

It's deuce—forty all. Dave's shot hits the net and topples over. His advantage. He serves the next ball straight and hard down the middle of the court. It's just outside the line, but both of us see it go in.

"Ace!" I shout. "That's your game, Dave!"

Dave goes insane. He spins around in circles, punching the air and whispering, "Yes! Yes! Yes!"

"You beat me, Dave!"

"I whipped you, Will!"

"You creamed me, Dave!"

Dave laughs loudly. "You know who I am, Will? I'm Pistol Pete!"

I act dumb. "Who's that, Dave?"

"Pete Sampras! The greatest. Thirteen Grand Slams. Seven Wimbledons. Slam-dunk smash! And you know who you are, don't you, Will?"

"Andre Agassi?"

"That's right, Will! The bald badger! The choker! Remember what Ken said?"

"Once a choker, always a choker."

Dave spins his wheelchair in circles again.

"Once a choker, always a choker! Once a choker, always a choker!"

Andre Agassi is one of those tennis players with a near-perfect technique. His ground shots are brilliant, both forehand and backhand. His volleys and serve could do with some work, maybe, but according to Ken, his main weakness is in his head. A choker is someone who can't perform under pressure. When the going gets tough, he falls apart.

"But you're not really a choker, are you, Will?"

"No, Dave. And neither is Andre Agassi."

"But I *am* Pistol Pete, aren't I!"

Mia

Will Holland is standing by the gate after school, talking to the seventh-grade girls. Doesn't he have anything better to do? Hasn't his felt-tipped pen run out of ink yet?

"Mia!" he says, as I limp out the gate. "How's your ankle?"

"Getting better," I say curtly.

"What's the difference between a viola and an onion?"

I don't answer.

"Nobody cries when they chop up a viola."

"Is that supposed to cheer me up?"

"Sorry, I just thought—"

"You could have told me, you know."

"About the tennis game? I tried to tell you."

"Why didn't you tell me *before* the game?"

"I wanted to surprise you."

"You wanted to *impress* me, you mean. You're just like all the other boys, Will Holland. If you want a girlfriend who sits in the crowd and cheers for you, then lets you write your name all over her body, good luck! Girls are like cattle to you, aren't they, Will? You think if you see your name on them, you must own them. Maybe you should start using a branding iron, to save time!"

Will

Dave loves me taking him to the park. He loves it almost as much as going to the pool. It's not the grass and the trees that Dave loves. It's not the playground or the little lake with the children feeding the ducks. It's not the winding gravel path where he can race ahead of me or the girls jogging past in their skin-tight bicycle shorts. What Dave really loves about the park are the chin-up bars. And the reason Dave loves them so much is that he can do more chin-ups than me.

After pushing a wheelchair for three years, Dave's arms and shoulders have beefed right up. He positions the wheelchair under the lowest bar, pulls himself up off his seat, and away he goes: "Ten . . . twenty . . . thirty . . ."

Dave insists that I stand by and watch him. He has a terrifying look of determination on his face, and his tongue sticks out slightly from the side of his mouth.

". . . Fifty-five . . . sixty . . ."

As Dave gets closer to one hundred he breaks out in a sweat and slows right down. It's like watching a champion weight lifter psych himself between lifts.

"Ninety-two . . . ninety-three . . . ninety-four . . ."

Mostly, when Dave gets to a hundred, he quits. More important to Dave than a new personal best is to see me on the chin-up bar, trying to make forty. As anyone will tell you, doing forty chin-ups is no mean effort, but that doesn't stop Dave from laughing at me.

"Thirty-four . . . thirty-five . . . thirty-six . . ."

"Come on, Will! We haven't got all day!"

"Thirty-seven . . . thirty-eight . . ."

"What are you, Will? A weed?"

"Thirty-nine! That's it, Dave! I give up!"

"That's hopeless, Will! You didn't even make forty!"

I get a drink of water, then sit down on the grass to rest. I don't know if it's the endorphins or the testosterone, but after Dave beats me at chin-ups, he always wants to talk about girls.

"Are you still in love with her, Will?"

"Who, Dave?"

"You know who, Will. That girl who doesn't like horses."

"Her name's Mia. I never said I was in love with her, Dave. I said I liked her."

"Isn't she your girlfriend anymore?"

"She never was, Dave."

"But you still like her, Will, even if you don't love her?"

"I still do, Dave. But there are girls you have as girl-friends and girls you have as friends, I guess."

"Have you got a *new* girlfriend, Will? Can I have your old girlfriend?"

"It's not up to me, Dave. You'd have to ask her."

"I'm not going to ask her, Will! I didn't mean it like that."

"I know, Dave."

Dave looks up at the trees. "What *is* love anyway, Will?"

"I don't know, Dave."

According to *The Encyclopedia of Tennis*, "love" is a zero score, and a "love game" is a blitz.

Mia

My father is working late, so Mom and I eat dinner without him—fish and chips again. Mom was always a pretty good cook, but lately she's been losing interest. The carpet needs vacuuming. There are coffee cups in the living room, and the laundry basket is overflowing. Harriet has started digging up the garden.

My father is having an affair with a woman half his age. Will Holland is signing his name all over seventh-grade girls. Is it possible to still be interested in someone, even when they're not interested in you? Is it possible that I am like my mom?

After dinner, I go to my room to practice my viola. The viola is a forgotten instrument, and tonight I feel like a forgotten girl. In fifty years' time, my bedroom will look like Miss Havisham's. All the clocks will have stopped, and everything will be covered in dust and cobwebs. I will be an old spinster with cold, flaky skin and a broken heart, sitting here playing my viola in my faded bridal gown, while rats devour the wedding cake. I will play the same sad song—*tranquillo e molto triste*—over and over, thinking about the young man who came to my window and how I told him to go away.

The front door opens, and I hear my father's footsteps go down the hall. I open the door just a crack, and I can smell it—the unmistakable scent of a young woman's perfume. How could my mother not notice it?

"Your dinner is in the oven," she says.

"I've already eaten," he replies.

Will

"It's not whether you win or lose," Ken says, "because losing is not an option."

And he's right. Playing tennis is fun. It feels good when you hit the ball properly. You feel the spring in the racket and you hear that *ping* as the ball connects with it. But what it's all about is beating the other guy and being the best. Otherwise, you might as well be hitting against a brick wall.

I am in the closet. My bedroom door is locked. It's dark and quiet and comfortable—I know I won't be interrupted. I was going to make a phone call. I was going to call Mia up and explain about the seventh-grade girls. But then I figured, what's the point? How do I know I would actually be able to say it, when it came to the crunch?

When I was young, I read the books about Narnia— where children went into a wardrobe and found another world. But the only world I want to find is the real world— a world where I can talk to Mia without feeling like a total idiot.

Andre Agassi was a choker, but then he got over it. Maybe someone helped him, or maybe he just got sick of losing. The fact is, now Andre Agassi knows how to play under pressure. He wins the important games. He knows how to talk to girls.

Mia

Renata is taking Vanessa's side—it's official. I don't know what Vanessa said to her, but I swear she must have said something. I can tell by the way Renata smiles at me. It's a Vanessa smile. At first I thought it meant, I can't talk to you, or I don't know what to say. But now I know it means, Don't talk to me. It's official.

Our seat has been taken over by other girls—girls without problems. Now, instead of sitting down at lunchtime, Vanessa and Renata walk around the school. If they see me, they smile, but the smiles mean Don't talk to us, and they keep on walking. Renata turns around and gives me another smile: *I'm really sad about what's happened between you and Vanessa.* And I smile sadly back at her: *But what's happened between you and me?*

When boys fight, they make threats and push each other around. They organize a time and place, then punch the living daylights out of each other. They get a few bruises, and it's over. When girls fight, it's much more nasty. Girl fights can go on for years. They can make you feel rejected. They can make you feel like dirt.

I hate Vanessa, but I can't wait until Renata goes away.

Will

The next tennis tournament is way out west, four hours away by car. It is a rainy Thursday afternoon, and Dave wants to play "I spy."

"I spy with my little eye," he says, "something beginning with P."

"Puddles?"

"No, Will."

"Passenger?"

"No, Will!"

"Pouring? Pouring rain."

"Will! *Pouring rain* is not a very good guess."

"What is it, Dave?"

"Do you give up, Will?"

"I give up, Dave."

"Are you sure, Will?"

"I'm sure, Dave."

Dave is laughing now. "It's me! Pistol Pete!"

"Good one, Dave!"

"It's your turn, Will."

"Hey, Dave," I say. "What's the difference between a viola and a trampoline?"

"I give up, Will."

"You take your shoes off to jump on a trampoline."

"I don't get it, Will. What's a viola?"

Mia

After school, to avoid Vanessa, I walk home the long way, through the park. There are daisies on the grass and blossoms on the trees. Compared to school, it is like another world. Without my crutches, I limp across the open lawn, between the tall trees with their ghostly gray papery bark, peeling off into strips. Underneath they are smooth and vulnerable-looking. I have lost my two best friends. I know it's part of life to shed your skin and let go of your troubles, but I can't help feeling sorry for those trees.

I am hobbling along, deep in my thoughts, when *whack!* From out of nowhere, something hard and sharp hits me in the back of the head. Overhead, I see a magpie swooping toward me. In shock and pain, I duck, and it veers away. Instead of returning to its treetop, the disgusting creature spins around and dives again! It's evil! Why is it picking on me?

With tears streaming down my face, I run for cover. My ankle buckles under me, and I fall to the ground, sobbing.

Will

The tournament is a knockout competition—six single-set rounds played over three days, and you have to keep winning to stay in it. My first game is against a complete outsider. That's how they do the draw—the top-seeded players play off against the new ones first, to avoid an early upset.

By Friday morning the rain has cleared. The court is damp, but fine to play on. The crowd looks like friends and relatives of my opponent. It doesn't feel much like a tournament—it feels more like a practice match. My opponent is shorter than me and slightly overweight. He is eating a

packet of Cheetos when they introduce us. I shake his pow-
dery yellow hands, and he smiles with bits of Cheetos
between his teeth. Biomechanics tells me he will be slow
around the court and not too confident with his overhead shots. It should be a comfortable way to start the
tournament. I can ease myself in and practice my ground
strokes.

I win the toss and elect to serve. I decide to do a Pete
Sampras and open with an ace to establish dominance.
When I look at Mr. Cheetos, standing there on the base-
line, I feel like Pete Sampras. I feel like Number One.

"Go, Will!" Dave yells from the crowd, as I throw the ball
high and hit it as hard as I can.

It's long. "Fault!" says the umpire.

For my second serve, I try the same thing again. Not the
wisest move, I know, but not unreasonable, under the circumstances. I throw the ball high and hit it hard into the
net for a double fault.

"Love fifteen," says the umpire.

"Come on," Ken mutters. "Pull your head in."

My next serve, I decide, will be a return to form. I will
focus on my technique and do it by the book. I don't resent
Ken saying what he did. It *is* his job, after all. I throw the
ball lower this time and hit it with less power, but it doesn't
feel right, and I hit it long again. It rattles me, and my second serve is a lollipop, aimed at avoiding another double
fault. Cheetos has no trouble putting it away.

"Love thirty," says the umpire.

My next serve connects well. It travels fast down the center, swinging away from Cheetos's backhand. It is such a relief to see it go in, it catches me off guard when Cheetos returns it.

"Love forty."

It is break point, and the match has barely started. When I look at Dave, his face says it all: *You're not a choker, Will. Don't be a choker.*

Desperately, I try to do what Ken has always told me. "Concentrate on technique. Don't listen to your head." But just looking at the ball as I hold it in my hands, nothing seems familiar anymore. I throw the ball in the air and catch it again. Someone coughs. I serve nervously, and Cheetos puts it away. The crowd cheers. Cheetos has broken my serve and won the first game.

Ken is shaking his head. Dave can hardly believe it.

I am in trouble.

We change ends, and Cheetos serves. His serves are nothing special, but his follow-ups are good. Slowly but surely, I settle down, and my confidence returns. I am playing better shots now, but the damage has already been done. Cheetos holds onto his serve, and I hold mine. After playing for almost an hour, the score is five games to four, with Cheetos serving, this time for the match.

The crowd is excited now. They can smell victory. A part of me wants to give up right then and there. Let them have their stupid tournament. Another part of me wants to win, just to spite them.

Cheetos wins the first point from a serve that clips the top of the net. It looks as though even God is on his side. His second serve is very ordinary, so I hit the ball long and hard to his backhand. It lands in, for sure, but the umpire calls it out. It's hometown favoritism—the umpire is on the payroll.

"No way!" I tell him.

"Who do you think you are?" he replies. "John McEnroe?"

Cheetos serves an ace after that. A killer serve that comes from out of nowhere.

"Forty love," announces the umpire. "Set point."

It is set point and match point. Cheetos has three chances in a row. If I lose another shot, I'm toast.

I lob Cheetos's next serve nervously into the air. The ball floats way up high and comes down right in the center of the court—a sitter. Cheetos lets it bounce, then moves in for the kill. I can hardly bear to watch, but in his excitement he mis-hits into the net.

"Forty fifteen."

"That's it, Will!" Dave shouts. "You can do it!"

I look at my racket and try to calm my nerves. I've been in this situation before, of course, but I've never felt so nervous. I look at Cheetos and the grim determination in his face. It's just a stupid tennis game, I keep telling myself. It's hardly worth getting upset about.

Cheetos serves hard and wide, trying for an ace. He serves the same again and does a double fault—his first for the match. He is feeling the pressure, too.

"Forty thirty."

Cheetos has one more set point up his sleeve. I have one more point to survive. It will be deuce—forty all—and I can stage a comeback. I am fitter and more experienced than Cheetos, so I should have more in reserve. It will all be so easy, if only I can win the next point. I could go on to win the match. I could win the whole damn tournament, if only I can survive the next point.

I notice a girl in the crowd with a pierced belly button. It makes me think of Vanessa. Does Mia have a pierced belly button? I wonder.

"Concentrate!" I tell myself.

Cheetos serves, and I return it hard. He hits a nice back-hand, and I respond with a neat half-volley. Cheetos runs in to the net too soon, but he manages to jump up and get it. Now he is caught out, dead center. All I have to do is hit the ball past him or lob it over his head. Instead, in a flash of anger, I hit it straight at him with all the power I have. I am aiming for his head—I want to hit him, even hurt him. Cheetos sees the ball coming and gets his racket up just in time. He is protecting himself, more than playing a shot, but the ball rebounds off his racket and somehow goes over the net. It's a no-brainer—impossible to get—so I don't even try.

Cheetos goes down on his knees in victory—the biggest cliché in the book. His family runs onto the court and lifts him up—the second biggest cliché. I feel like going over and reminding them that it *is* just the first round of the tournament, after all.

It's the first round of the tournament, and I am already out. When I look at how happy the crowd is, I feel like crying. Everyone loves a winner. No one loves a loser.

"Useless!" I shout in sudden anger, smashing my racket hard against the ground.

Mia

It is eight o'clock, and my father has just come home from work. He is late, as usual, because he was having a drink with his colleagues, he says, which of course means he's been out with *her*, as usual. Have they been out for a drink or off for a quickie at the local motel? It doesn't matter which. Mom is acting as if nothing strange has happened, and I am expected to go along with it.

After a hard day of cutting people open and stitching them back up again, a round of drinks with his colleagues and/or a hot half-hour in the motel spa, my father is spent. After briefly consulting his wine guide, he descends into the cellar and emerges with a bottle in his hand and a glint in his eye. He comes into the living room, where I am practicing my viola. He slumps down in his chair, loosens his tie, and uncorks the bottle. He pours himself a glass, holds it up to the light, sniffs it, and takes a cautious sip.

"Mmm . . . hits the spot," he says.

I continue to practice while my father sits in his chair, sipping and nodding. Pretty soon he has kicked off his shoes and is staring into his glass.

"Just what I needed."

I smile at Dad, and he smiles at me.

"Vivaldi," he says. "*Danze Pastorale?*"

"*Allegro non molto.*"

He smiles sentimentally. "It's been a few years since I played it."

I nod uncertainly, and my dad's smile fades.

"Would you mind terribly if I put on a CD?" he says. "It's been a long day."

"Are you saying you want me to go and practice in my room?"

"Would you mind, darling?"

I pack up and leave. My father is already scanning his CD collection. As I shut my bedroom door, I hear the music start. It is fast and loud—too fast for my dad. He must have got it from *her*.

I want my bedroom to be a cold dark cave. I want black walls, black curtains, and black windows. I want to paint the glass to keep out the sunlight. I want headless dolls, shredded books, and a pillow stuffed with magpie feathers.

I set up my music stand and open my sheet music. The second movement of *Spring* sounds so stupid and pointless. Ms. S. says the viola part is meant to sound like a dog barking—how offensive! It says *pianissimo sempre,* but instead I play *matali*—attacking the strings until the bow is shredded horsehair. Outside my window, Harriet starts barking— Ms. S. would be impressed. As her barking gets louder, so does my playing. I am not listening to the notes anymore, or even to the rhythm. All I can hear is the *sound*, getting louder and wilder. It's all about spring—paranoid magpies protecting their nests and witchy Vanessa, flirting with Will. And I am a mad gypsy woman, dancing on hot coals— *molto espressivo*—faster and faster, wilder and wilder . . .

Then I hear my father, knocking on my bedroom door.

"Mia! Can you tone it down a bit? It sounds like a dying cat!"

I stop playing. With tears in my eyes I stand there with my viola tucked under my chin, listening to his footsteps going back down the hall.

Then Mom says, "Surely you're not going out again!"

I put down my viola. Suddenly I feel cold and hard as steel.

When I open my bedroom door, the house is quiet. Dad is in the bathroom, and Mom is watching TV. I pick up the viola, open the front door, and walk out the gate. Dad's four-wheel drive is parked outside in the street. No one sees me as I lay the viola under the back tire.

As my father is leaving, I stand in the doorway and wave good-bye. I hear the viola crack and splinter into firewood. It's an awful, tearing sound, like the end of all music, like all the viola's future notes dying before they were even born. It's the sound of something fragile and beautiful being run over by something big and heavy. It's the sound of my heart breaking, and Dad doesn't even hear it. He has that same CD on—the one that *she* has given him. The one that is too fast and loud.

When the car is gone, I kneel down and pick up the pieces of the smashed viola. One by one, I put them in the case, even the tiniest splinter. When I go back inside the house, Mom is there on the couch with a glass of wine in her hand and the remote control on her lap. When she sees the viola case, she smiles briefly, and I smile back.

It's easy to smile when you don't feel a thing.

four

Will

"It's not the end of the world, Will."

"No, Dave. It's not the end of the world."

"You know where you lost it, Will? Your lousy drop-shots. They need more top-spin, to make the ball drop. Drop-shot, get it?"

"Thanks for the advice, Dave."

"Don't worry, Will. It's not the end of the world."

"You're right, Dave. It's not the end of the world."

"Why'd you break your racket, Will? Wasn't it a very good one?"

"It wasn't the racket, Dave. It was me."

"Were you angry, Will? You looked angry."

"I should have won, Dave."

"But you're not angry with me, are you, Will?"

"Of course not, Dave."

"Because it's not the end of the world, is it, Will?"

"No, Dave. It's not the end of the world."

"Can I have your racket, Will?"

"Why do you want my racket, Dave?"

"Because it's broken, Will. You don't need it anymore."

The drive home from the tournament is the longest four hours of my life. Dave won't shut up, and Ken barely says a word—it is impossible to guess what he is thinking.

I spy with my little eye something beginning with L.

Loser, Ken. Your son is a big-time loser.

Mia

The smashed viola is in its case under my bed—*segreto*—hidden under blankets. Even so, I sleep badly, waking every hour just to check that it's still there. I dream about my father finding it. He undoes the latch and lifts the top, but instead of viola pieces the case is full of dead flowers. I wake in fright to find the gypsy woman sitting on the end of my bed.

"Darlink!" she says. "It was just a bad dream."

"What can I do?" I whimper. "How can I stop him from finding out?"

The gypsy woman takes out a pack of cards and begins to shuffle them.

"You could lock it up in chains and bury it in the backyard," she says. "You could run away from home and come back when you're rich and famous."

"How could I get rich and famous?"

The gypsy woman begins to lay out the cards on my bed.

"Drugs? Prostitution?" she says. "Become an actress?"

"I could say it was stolen. Is it insured? Should I ask my dad?"

But the gypsy woman seems more interested in her cards.

"What about me?" I say. "Aren't you going to read my future?"

The gypsy woman picks up a card and turns it over—the ace of hearts.

"No, darlink," she says. "I'm playing solitaire."

Next morning, at breakfast, I smile at my father, and he smiles back. The toast pops up, and Mom brings it over. She asks Dad if he wants another cup of tea. He says, "Thank you." It's all very normal, just like a happy family should be. It's all wrong.

"How's the Vivaldi going?" he asks, and I choke on my mouthful of cornflakes.

"Pretty good."

"I'm looking forward to the concert," he says.

I try to smile as the terror returns. I'm smiling so hard, my cheeks feel like they're going to crack. What if he asks to see the viola? What if he wants to play it?

I stand up and make a lame excuse.

"I'm taking Harriet for a walk."

Instead of being even slightly suspicious, my father turns the page of his newspaper. I don't need a padlock and chain to stop him finding my smashed viola. I could leave it on the table right in front of him, and he'd never even think of looking.

Will

"Seventeen . . . eighteen . . . nineteen . . ."

According to *The Encyclopedia of Tennis*, probably the most dramatic and widely seen rally of all time was the nineteen-stroke set-point duel played by Agassi and Sampras in the 1995 U.S. Open final, which Sampras ended with a killer backhand to take the opening set.

". . . Thirty-six . . . thirty-seven . . ."

According to the *Encyclopedia*, there have been other, much longer rallies in the history of the game, including one that went for twenty-nine minutes and notched up six hundred and forty-three strokes! I wonder how long the game took. Who knows? Maybe they're still playing.

". . . Forty-nine . . . fifty!"

Dave claps and cheers as I drop to the ground, nursing my poor hands. Instead of his usual air of superiority, today he has genuine respect in his voice.

"Geez, Will! That's your best ever by far!"

My palms are hot and red, with puffy white lumps of skin already starting to appear. When I show them to Dave, he looks worried.

"Does it hurt, Will? It looks sore."

"It stings a bit, Dave."

"You'll get blisters, Will. You won't be able to play tennis."

"Then maybe I should do more, Dave?"

Dave smiles uncertainly. "Is that why you did it, Will? So you don't have to play tennis? Is that why you broke your racket, Will? What will Ken say, Will?"

"I don't care what Ken says."

"Are you giving up, Will? Have you finished being a champion?"

"I don't know, Dave."

"Does that mean we won't be rich, Will? Does it mean we won't live in the Caribbean? Does it mean we won't have a swimming pool?"

"I don't know, Dave."

"Ken is going to kill you, Will."

"It's my life, Dave."

"He's going to kill you, Will!"

"It's your turn, Dave."

As Dave begins his chin-up marathon, I see a girl in the distance, chasing her dog. She is too far away to recognize, but the dog looks familiar. I can't take my eyes off them. It's the way the girl is running—her biomechanics are very familiar.

"Keep going, Dave," I say. "I'll be back in a minute."

Mia

"I'm in trouble, Harriet. I don't know what to do. I'll have to leave home and become a wandering gypsy woman. You can come with me. We can perform in the city. You can do dog tricks, jump through hoops and stand on your hind legs. We could open the viola case, and people would give us money. Harriet the Wonder Dog, we'll call you. I'll make you a little red cape."

But Harriet the Wonder Dog isn't interested in fame and glory. All she cares about is sniffing for doggy smells. I tell her to sit, and she sits with her tail wagging. As soon as I pat her, she's up again, wrapping her leash around my legs as she runs around in circles sniffing the grass.

A gypsy with a smashed viola and a performing dog who can't sit still? It might be hard to make a living.

All through my childhood I wanted a dog, so why did my parents wait so long? If Harriet were older and wiser, she would understand what was happening in my life. She would know how to sit, beg, lie down, roll over. I could let her off the leash, and she wouldn't get run over. What was it with my parents? Didn't they trust me to look after a dog? Or was it the fleas in the carpet and dog turds on the lawn?

My parents are so boring and predictable. The way they speak is so polite and cheerful. The way they smile is so reassuring. It's crazy to think that everyone should always be smiling. If you're always expected to feel happy, what hope have you got of finding out how you really feel? Feeling angry or sad or nervous or scared is just a part of life. You have to feel the bad things to know that you're alive. You have to feel bad to know when you're feeling good. People who always smile are scared of admitting how they really feel. They think feelings are like puppy dogs—if you don't keep them on a leash, they might run away and never come back.

"Sit, girl!"

Harriet sits and scratches her ear with her back leg as I unhook the chain from her collar. She tilts her head and looks at the leash in my hand.

"Stay, girl!"

I take a few steps away from her, crouch down, and call her.

"Here, girl!"

Harriet leaps toward me, then slips through my fingers

and runs away across the park. When I call out for her to come back, she runs even faster.

Will

Mia's dog runs ahead of her, weaving and dodging as if it's part of some game. I try to cut her off, but she swerves at the last moment, and I almost collide with Mia. Puffing and taking deep breaths, we watch the little beagle tear across the grass to where Dave is hanging from the chin-up bar. Taken by surprise as the dog leaps up and paws him, Dave loses his grip and falls to the ground. Mia puts her hand to her mouth, but I can't help laughing. The dog has Dave pinned to the ground and is licking his face and hair.

And Dave loves it.

Mia runs over and pulls Harriet off as I help my brother back into his wheelchair. Normally, Dave would be embarrassed about meeting a pretty girl for the first time. But because of Harriet, his excitement has overcome any shyness. He calls the dog to him and lifts her up into his wheelchair. Harriet sits there, uncomfortable and uncertain, as Dave scratches her back and pulls on her ears. When I introduce Mia, he looks her up and down.

"Will told me all about you," he says.

Mia laughs. "What did he say?"

"He said you were his friend, not his girlfriend."

"I see," says Mia. "How many chin-ups can you do?"

"A hundred and eight!" says Dave proudly. "How many can you do?"

"Maybe one, if I'm lucky."

Dave laughs, then frowns suddenly.

"Will did fifty!" he says. "That's because he doesn't want to play tennis."

With Harriet held captive on his lap, Dave gives Mia a blow-by-blow account of the tennis match, complete with coaching tips, fitness advice, and brotherly sympathy. There is nothing I can do or say. The more I try to interrupt them, the more determined they are to talk about me. I can see that Mia likes Dave and Dave likes Mia. It isn't long before he starts babbling.

"Will got me a book called *The Encyclopedia of Tennis*. I'm up to page 460. You can borrow it when I'm finished. It's got everything in it. It's got the fifty greatest players of all time and the scores of all the big games. I play tennis, too. What about you? Do you play tennis?"

"Mia plays in the orchestra, Dave. She plays the viola."

Dave nods knowingly. "Will knows lots of jokes about violas. Tell her, Will. Tell her the one about the smashed-up viola."

When I look at Mia, she has tears in her eyes.

Dave looks up at the trees, embarrassed.

"No more viola jokes," I say.

Harriet walks in front of us, towing Dave like a Roman chariot while Mia and I follow behind like centurions in full armor. In this strange procession we walk around the park together without talking. It's not that uncomfortable silence that comes from not knowing what to say. It's a silence that comes from not wanting to be nosy. I want to ask Mia about her father, but I get the feeling she's not ready to tell me yet.

"How's the orchestra?" I ask.

Mia smiles grimly. "What do you throw a drowning violist?" she says. "Her viola."

Mia

At the lockers, Vanessa smiles at me and I smile back. Her smile says, *My life is perfect.* And my smile says, *Well, my life is perfect, too.* Her smile says, *My life is MORE perfect than your life.* And my smile says, *If your life is so perfect, then why do you need to smile like that?* Her smile says, *Actually, I'm smiling out of pity because you are so pathetic.* And my smile says, *I'm not scared of you, Vanessa. There is nothing you can say to upset me.*

"Did you know?" says Vanessa. "Renata's gone to Europe."

My face drops, and my brave smile slips sadly away.

To avoid another smile-off with Vanessa, I sneak into the music room and sit there in the half-darkness, surrounded by empty chairs and music stands. With my eyes closed, I sit perfectly still with my hands in my lap, while my head spins with unhappy questions. How could Renata have left without saying good-bye? What did Vanessa tell her about me? And why did Renata believe it? Who else might Vanessa talk to, and what might she say? That my bedroom looks like a doll's house? That I wear a size 34B bra?

What might she say to Will? And would he believe her?

As the minutes tick away, the questions fade, and my head slowly stops spinning. I don't care what Vanessa told Renata or what she says to Will. I don't care what Will thinks. I don't care how many young women my father sees. I don't care how many seventh-grade girls Will signs his name on. I don't care what breast size boys prefer or what Vanessa's smiles mean.

When I look around at the empty chairs I imagine an invisible orchestra, playing with the perfect rhythm of silence. The rhythm fills the empty room and starts ringing in my ears. Imagine a world without silence. Without silence there could never be music.

Suddenly, the door to the music room opens. The lights go on and in walks Ms. Stanway.

"Mia!" She looks surprised.

I stand up, embarrassed. "Sorry. I was just—"

"How are you finding the Vivaldi?" asks Ms. S.

I don't know what to say. "My viola," I say. "I left it at home."

Like a metronome, Ms. Stanway wags a pale finger at me, but then her face softens.

"Don't worry," she says. "I'm sure we can borrow one."

I burst into tears.

"It was my father's!" I sob. "My dad is going to kill me!"

Will

There is no announcement at school assembly. Announcements are for winners. Losers get ignored. When I walk down the corridor, no one pats me on the back. The teachers are all too busy. The seventh-grade girls look away, embarrassed.

It's not whether you win or lose . . . because losing is not an option.

Yorick has been reading about the space-time continuum. "Time travel will never be possible," he says. "No one from the future has ever come back to visit us."

"Who would ever want to?" I say.

Winners get trophies and their names in the Hall of Fame. They get free tennis rackets, guest spots on talk radio, and their photos on boxes of breakfast cereal. Losers get forgotten. They turn into ghosts and spend the rest of eternity arguing about whether the ball was in or out.

Thank you for calling Losers Anonymous. Please leave your name and number, your personal hopes and dreams, and we won't remember to phone you back. . . .

At lunchtime I see Bryce, the arm-wrestling champion, preparing to defend his title against the challenger at the head of the line. It's a stupid game, but somehow, as a spectator sport, it's got me. Because you have to keep one arm behind your back and both feet on the ground, because there is no shouldering or punching allowed, it becomes a game of strategies and lightning reflexes. To win you have to predict your opponent's moves and use them against him, the way Yorick does on the chessboard.

I watch the next challenger put up a brave fight, until eventually Bryce has him on his knees. Bryce looks pretty ordinary, though. Apart from having strong arms and a height advantage, there is nothing very impressive about him. His movements are slow and obvious. He is top-heavy—all his strength comes from shoulder height. According to the laws of biomechanics, he would easily lose his balance if he ever got caught off guard.

I could beat him.

According to *The Encyclopedia of Tennis*, a "wild card" is an underranked star who decides to enter the tournament at the last minute.

"Holland!" Bryce calls, as I take up my place in the line. "Finally come to get your ass kicked?"

"Actually, I was planning on kicking *your* ass."

Bryce laughs. "You're going to need more than a strong serving arm, buddy."

Bryce orders the other guys in the line to make way for me, which they do without complaining. Everyone is interested, suddenly, as if it's a title fight.

I step up to face Bryce. He is taller than me, but I have a longer reach.

"You know the rules?" he says.

"I think so."

"First to move his feet or first to give up. You ready?"

I look around at the guys who are watching. I can tell

from their faces they are waiting to see me lose. Farther away, leaning against the fence, I see Vanessa is watching, too. Suddenly, it feels like the whole school is watching.

The fight is over in a flash. I know Bryce will try to strike first, and I am ready for him. As his arm comes shooting toward me, I grab hold of his wrist and pull it, leaning sideways to upset his balance. As Bryce falls, he grabs my arm and twists it hard. I feel a sharp, stabbing pain in my elbow, but I know I'm the winner.

Will Holland—the new school champion!

The other guys nod their heads in approval, and Bryce vows to get me next time for sure. The next guy in the line looks like a pushover, but my elbow hurts, so I forfeit the fight, and he gets the title.

Vanessa signals to me, and I wander over, rubbing my sore arm.

"Impressive!" she says, though I can't tell if she means it or not.

When she sees I'm in pain, Vanessa smiles sympathetically and reaches out to touch the sore spot. "Poor baby," she says.

I'm still wary, but I like the feel of her soft, cool fingers on my skin.

"My personal trainer?" I say.

"At your service," she says.

According to *The Encyclopedia of Tennis*, "service" is the act of putting the ball in play, and any motion—underhand or other—is permitted.

Mia

There they are—Vanessa and Will—together in broad day-
light. She is touching his arm, and he is letting her! Will
and Vanessa, being intimate and physical for all the world
to see. She is massaging his arm, and he is letting her! She
is using both hands, and he is loving it! Will sits down, and
Vanessa kneels behind him. She leans against him, rubbing his shoulders. He rolls his head around like he is in
heaven. For a moment it looks like they are actually going
to *do it* right here, in front of the whole school!

It's a truly sickening sight.

I'm in shock. I know people do *do it*. I *have* seen movies
with people doing it. I *have* read books. Some days, it seems
like everyone is doing it wherever you look, even though
no one you actually know has ever done it. It's everywhere,
but invisible. It happens all the time, but it's hard to
imagine.

It should be easy enough, to imagine doing it. You can
imagine doing anything with anyone, so why should *it* be
any different? I don't know what boys imagine when they
imagine doing it, but when I imagine doing it, I imagine
almost everything but the actual *it*. I can get a clear picture
of what happens before and after, but when it comes to
during, I tend to leave out the gory details—not that the
details are gory. It's just that imagining things sometimes
makes them less interesting, if you know what I mean.

And now, here I am, being forced to imagine Will and
Vanessa doing it. Maybe not today, maybe not here, in front

of all the school. But when and where are obviously not going to be a major problem for them.

I feel sick in my stomach.

For the rest of that afternoon, I drift along in a kind of daze. I imagine *it* happening everywhere. Insects are out in the garden, doing it. Beetles are crawling into holes and doing it. In the biology room, the preserved rats are trying to climb up out of their jars to do it. In media studies, the newsreaders are doing it during the ad breaks.

Finally, the bell goes. I grab my bag and manage to get out the gate before the whole school starts doing it. Walking home, there are people doing it in cars. People are sneaking into stores to do it. Busloads are going home to do it, and the ones in the backseat can't even wait that long.

That night, after dinner, the phone rings and I answer it. For a moment I hope it might even be Will. But it isn't Will—it's *her*. The girl who is *doing it* with my dad.

"Is that Mia?" she says, sweetly. "It's Tina, a friend of your father's. Is he there? Could I have a quick word?"

I am dumbstruck. How does she know my name? Who does she think she is, calling like this, telling me her name and saying she's *a friend* of my father's? I don't want to know her name. I don't want to know anything about her. And why is she calling, on *my* phone, in *my* house, to speak to *my* father!

What about my mom? Has the whole world gone mad?

I can think of a few quick words that Tina could have. Instead, I put down the receiver and call out in a loud voice, "Dad! Your girlfriend's on the phone. . . . I think she feels like doing it!"

Will

At lunchtime I see Vanessa Webb standing alone by the back gate.

"I've run out of smokes," she says. "Want to run out to the store with me?"

"Sure."

We wait until the coast is clear, then we sneak out the gate and around the corner into a side street. We are walking fast and laughing nervously. When a police car goes past, Vanessa takes my hand and squeezes it hard.

"Partners in crime," she laughs.

At the deli Vanessa buys her smokes, then we go and sit out of sight in the parking lot at the back. When Vanessa offers me a smoke, I turn her down.

"Mr. Fitness," she says. "I almost forgot."

"Why do you smoke those things, anyway?"

Vanessa shrugs. "They help keep my weight down."

"You're in good shape," I say.

Vanessa smiles seductively. "How would you know what shape I'm in?"

She passes me her cigarette, and I take it between my fingers. It feels light and unfamiliar, like something I might easily crush or drop accidentally. It feels like a baton in some kind of intimate relay race. It feels like flirting.

"Are you going to smoke that thing or just look at it?"

I take a single drag on the cigarette. My lungs burn, and my head feels dizzy. It takes a major effort to keep my hand steady as I give it back to her.

Vanessa smokes her cigarette like a movie star. There is something very exciting about it, but also something not quite right—something not quite real. It's as if she is smoking the cigarette just to be seen. The director has started rolling the camera, and now Vanessa is smoking. It feels like that's why *I* am here—to watch Vanessa smoking her cigarette. When I zoom in for a close-up, I can see the pores of her skin. I can smell her warm, smoky breath. It would be so easy to lean across and kiss her. I'm sure it's in the script . . .

. . . *And* CUT!

A car pulls up, and Vanessa immediately stubs out her cigarette. The principal winds down her window and looks at both of us, but it's me she speaks to.

"Will Holland!" she says. "What are *you* doing here?"

Mia

In class, I smile at the teacher: *Yes, I* AM *listening.* I smile at the canteen lady: *Yes, I know doughnuts are fattening, and yes, I want* THREE! I smile at Ms. S. when she kindly lends me a viola to keep until the concert: *Yes, but we* BOTH KNOW

I don't deserve it. At lunchtime, I wander the school grounds, smiling at the world: *Yes, it's a sunny day! Yes, I'm alone because I LIKE being alone.*

The truth is, inside I'm festering with poisonous thoughts about T***—that lipstick-smeared, adulterous home-wrecker whose name I can't even mention. I think about her husky voice on the phone—the equivalent of a fake smile. How *dare* she ask, "Is that Mia?" How *dare* she talk to me! How *dare* she use my name! And how *dare* he tell her my name! *Why* did he tell her? What *possible reason* could he have? *How* did he tell her? What *words* did he use?

"Her name is Mia, and I love her almost as much as I love you."

"Don't worry about Mia. She's a pushover."

"When we get married, I'm sure Mia will make a lovely bridesmaid."

I am walking and fuming and festering with black thoughts when I see something that stops me dead in my tracks. Up ahead Will and Vanessa are sneaking out the back gate—*sneaking* in full view—off for a not-so-secret rendezvous!

The world has gone completely mad. No one cares about how other people feel. Everyone does what they like and gets away with it. All the rules are broken, including the one about not turning on your friends.

Will

After school we have detention. The principal sits at her desk, writing letters, while Vanessa and I exchange meaningful glances. Whenever she has to leave the room, we whisper desperate messages, like true partners in crime.

"How much longer?" I ask.

"Don't worry," she says. "It'll be over soon."

"What if she keeps us here till midnight?"

"She wants to go more than we do."

"How do you know?"

"This is your first time, isn't it?"

I nod.

Vanessa grins. "I've corrupted you, haven't I?"

Eventually, the principal tells us we're free to go. The corridors are empty, and our feet make squeaky sounds on the linoleum as we walk like pardoned prisoners toward the gate.

"I'm starving," says Vanessa. "Let's get something to eat."

Mia

When I get home from school, Mom is watching *The Bold and the Beautiful*. There's a glass of wine in her hand and an empty bottle on the table. Mom's clothes are crumpled and her makeup is smudged. There's nothing bold or beautiful about her.

"Are you okay?" I ask.

"I'm fine, sweetheart."

"You don't look okay."

Mom looks up at me with her sad, blurry eyes. There is so much she wants to tell me, but can't. There is so much she won't even admit to herself.

"Dad didn't come home last night, did he?"

Mom looks confused. "He was working late," she mumbles.

"You don't have to cover up for him!" I say. "And you don't have to protect me!"

"He's a good father," she says, meekly.

"Mom!" I scream. "How can you say that!"

I go to my room and slam the door. I open the viola case and stare at its awful contents. The pieces of wood are almost unrecognizable as a musical instrument. The viola began its life as a maple tree. It would have been chosen specially, maybe even specially grown. It would have been cut down and sawed up into sections. The best timber would have been slowly crafted—chiseled with great care and expertise, then fitted, sanded, and repeatedly varnished. It would have taken hours, weeks, months of delicate, skillful work. And the craftsman who made it would have loved it like a daughter.

Will

In the pizza place, Vanessa and I watch the guy rolling out the dough. He spins it on his hand, then lays it out on the aluminum dish and smears it with tomato paste. He scoops up a handful of cheese and spreads it around. He arranges the seafood, the salami and peppers, the ham and pineapple, the mushrooms and olives, then he puts the finished pizza onto the slow-moving conveyor belt.

"Is that eat-in or take-out?" he asks.

I look at Vanessa.

"Eat-in," she says.

We sit at a little table by the door, so that it almost could be take-out. If we changed our mind about eating in, we could pick up our pizza and step out into the street. Take-out means food you eat when you're hungry. Eating in means more than just the food. Eating in means it's a date. My first-ever date with a girl, and I am hopelessly unprepared.

Vanessa, on the other hand, is in her element. She orders something to drink for both of us. She studies the menu and tosses around other tricky words like *prosciutto* and *focaccia* as if she's part Italian.

"We should have ordered the Capricciosa," she says.

"I've never had a Quattro Stagioni," I say.

Vanessa looks worried, about either my bad pronunciation or my lack of pizza experience.

"Actually, this is only the"—I count on my fingers—"fifth pizza I've ever had."

"What?" Vanessa looks horrified.

"My dad says I'm not allowed to eat pizza."

"Your dad is weird."

"Ken has a master's degree in sports nutrition. He

majored in fat metabolism. Everything he eats is low-fat: low-fat yogurt, low-fat muffins, low-fat granola bars. He thinks pizza is evil."

Vanessa smiles. "It *is* evil."

Time passes. Seconds turn into minutes, and hours turn back into seconds. Vanessa puts the menu away and sips her soda. Light-years pass, and our pizza is lost forever inside the black-hole oven. Because it's a date, I feel I should say something. But because I've never been on a date before—and because the pizza is taking so long—I can't. I can't stop thinking that the conveyor belt must be broken and our pizza burned beyond recognition. The pizza guy is reading his newspaper. He's forgotten all about us.

"So," says Vanessa, finally. "How was it, being famous?"

"Pretty ordinary," I say.

"What was the best thing?"

I shrug my shoulders. "I got to go on a date with you?"

Vanessa laughs and looks me in the eye.

"I'm going to *stay* famous," she says, "and I'll do *whatever it takes*!"

Finally our pizza emerges from the oven, so the pizza guy slices it and brings it over. Vanessa takes a big slice in both hands and positions it above her open mouth like a sword swallower. She lowers the pizza and takes a bite, then pulls away, leaving a sagging bridge of melted mozzarella.

She looks so hungry, it's almost scary.

Mia

The hospital where my father works is in the city. My taxi drops me off outside the main entrance, then I catch the elevator up to the fifth floor: Ward C.

The nurse at reception smiles at me. "Can I help you?"

Has my dad ever *done it* with her, I wonder? Probably.

When I tell her who I am she says, "Dr. Foley? I think he's seeing someone."

"I'm sure he is."

I go and wait outside my dad's office until the door opens. A middle-aged woman steps out. She says "Thank you" as she closes the door behind her.

Has my dad just finished *doing it* with her as well?

Without knocking, I open the door and enter. My father is at his desk, searching for a file in his bottom drawer. He doesn't even look up.

"Yes?"

"You didn't come home last night."

"Mia!"

Dad stands up to welcome me. He tries to kiss me, but I pull away, so he shuts the door and sits back in his chair. As slowly and deliberately as I can, I place the closed viola case on the desk in front of him.

"How was orchestra practice?" he asks in his cheery doctor's voice.

"Where were you?"

Dad blinks.

I take a deep breath.

"Were you with . . . *her*? Were you with . . . your girlfriend?"

For a moment Dad looks flustered, but then he puts on his important doctor's face.

"Can we talk about this tonight? I have patients waiting."

I look at my father, the important doctor, sitting there behind his important doctor's desk, wearing his important doctor's suit. I look at his important doctor's hands, so clean and calmly folded on the desktop. They are surgeon's hands—hands that save lives. But they are also unfaithful hands—hands that like groping young women. In some countries, adulterers have their hands cut off.

"I don't want to talk about it," I say, trying to hold back my tears. "Not now. Not tonight. I didn't come here to talk about it. I came here to tell you to leave me and Mom alone. You're not a part of our family anymore. I don't *ever* want you to come home again!"

"You're upset," says Dad, holding out his hands to me. "I understand."

I shake my head. "You think if something is wrong, you can fix it. You think you can cut a hole in someone and take out the bad part. You think you can stitch them back up and everything will be okay, but you're wrong!"

My father stares in disbelief as I open the viola case and empty the shattered contents onto his desk.

"There are some things," I say, "that can never be fixed."

Will

It's after seven o'clock by the time I get home. Smelling of pizza, coffee, cigarettes, and Vanessa, I slip in the front door like a criminal—full of elaborate alibis and expecting the worst. But Ken's reaction is not what I expect. Instead of being angry, he smiles sympathetically.

"How's the elbow?" he says.

Besides his degree in nutrition, Ken has a certificate in sports massage from the Institute of Pain and Torture.

"Tell me if it hurts," he says, holding my shoulder and rotating my arm.

"It hurts."

"I spoke to a physiotherapist today. He recommended massage, hydrotherapy, and heat treatment, but if it's the ligaments, we should see a radiologist."

"Can't we just leave it alone?"

"If we don't get it fixed, we'll miss the whole summer."

I pull my arm away from him. "*We?* What about *me?* It's my elbow, isn't it? I'm the one who holds the racket. I'm the one who has to walk out there on the court. I say we leave it alone. I don't care how long it takes."

"You can't just give up," says Ken. "Not after all the hard work you've done."

He nods at the eight or nine tennis trophies on the bookshelf—serious little golden men like chocolate wrapped in tinfoil—as if they somehow mattered.

"There's more to life than playing tennis," I say. "You're not just my coach, Ken. You're also my dad, remember?"

Dave and Lyn appear in the doorway, looking concerned.

"Ken only wants you to be happy, Will," says Lyn, softly.

I look at the three of them, standing there, blocking my way with their endless patience and understanding. Ever since Dave's accident, there has been nothing but patience and understanding. In our family, Dave's accident is something you never talk about. It is something we never mention, not because it is too painful, but because it is understood. Dave's accident united our family in a way that other families could never be united. After the accident, it felt like us versus the rest of the world. We had to stick together—we had no choice. In our family you don't complain. If there is a problem, you work it out. Anger is out of line. Crying is not an option. For three years I have been brave and strong, like a third adult, helping to care for my disabled brother. But now, suddenly, I feel like throwing a tantrum.

"I'm not like Dave!" I shout. "I don't need you to plan my whole life! I don't need round-the-clock supervision!"

Lyn looks at Ken, and Ken looks at Lyn. I look at Dave, and Dave looks away. I feel ashamed of what I have said, but the damage is done. I don't know what to say to make it better.

five

Mia

There are no tears or big good-byes. I get home from school one day to find a note on the kitchen table: *Found a nice two-bedroom place. Call me—love, Dad.*

When I try calling my father on his cell phone, a recorded voice tells me the phone is either switched off or out of range. That figures.

Mom is very calm about it. She phones our lawyer, who recommends someone else, because he is already representing my dad. Mom writes down the number, thanks him, and hangs up.

"Well," she says, bravely. "What do you want for dinner?"

"I'll cook!" I say.

"There's not much in the fridge."

"Then I'll shop, too!"

Going to the supermarket is fine when you know what you want. But as a place for getting ideas, it is hopeless. Aisles 1 to 4 have no food whatsoever. Aisle 5 is full of breakfast cereal. Aisle 6 is cookies. Aisle 7 is soft drinks. Aisle 8 is candy. I am so worn out with looking by the time I get to Aisle 9, I grab the first thing I see. *Fettuccine Napoli. Boil pasta and add contents*, it says on the jar. *Simplistico!* I even buy a packet of Parmesan cheese for that extra gourmet touch.

When I get home, Mom is asleep on the couch, the TV is blaring, and there's another half-empty bottle of wine by her side. I go into the kitchen and get cracking. I fill a saucepan with water, add the pasta, and put it on the stove to heat. I set the table, then open the Parmesan cheese and put it in a bowl with a teaspoon, just like they do in Italian restaurants. By the time the pasta is cooked, it has soaked up most of the water. I add the Napoli sauce, stir it in with a big wooden spoon, and pop it on the table. *Perfecto!*

Mom is impressed. She says it's the best thing I've ever cooked, which is true enough, since it's also the only thing I've ever cooked.

"Such big helpings!" she says, as I am serving it up.

The pasta is a bit on the mushy side, but with the Parmesan it is almost perfecto. Satisfied with my first major cooking attempt, I clear the table and begin loading the dishwasher. Mom suggests we give the leftovers to Harriet as a special treat, but the spoiled little beagle-brat turns up her nose and won't touch it.

"How about dessert?" I say. "I could make crepes."

"No, let's go out for coffee and cake!" says Mom.

We go to a noisy café, where the menu is written up on a blackboard. We order our cakes, and suddenly Mom looks ten years younger, smiling as if I'm her best girlfriend.

"I suppose this has put you off getting married." She laughs.

"It's official," I say. "All men are evil."

"To chastity!" Mom replies, holding up her cup.

"Hang on! I thought we were talking about marriage, not sex."

Mom's jaw drops. "You haven't, have you?"

"No, and I'm not giving up before I even start."

"To true love, then."

We clink our coffee cups. "To true love."

Mom looks at me sheepishly. "Is there anyone you . . . ?"

"Not really."

"That boy who telephoned? Is he still—?"

"Not really."

"Are you at all—?"

"Not really."

"Does 'Not really' really mean 'Not really'?"

"Not really."

We laugh and talk. We hold hands and eat too much cake. We stay until the café closes, and neither of us mentions my father once.

When we get home, the house is in darkness. Everything is just as we'd left it, but Mom is suddenly on red alert.

"He's been here," she says. "I can smell that disgusting perfume."

She looks in the bedrooms. She checks the cupboards and bookshelves, but nothing is missing. Then she opens the door to the cellar. . . .

While we were out, my father has sneaked into the house and taken *all* the wine bottles. Not just a few favorite reds, we're talking about hundreds of bottles, some of them older than I am, all gone. Vanished into thin air. The wine cellar looks like a dungeon.

Mom goes totally bipolar. I've seen her cry before. I've seen her get angry. But I've never seen her rip up wedding photos and cut up my father's suits. I've never seen her throw his shoes onto the roof and bend his golf clubs. I've never heard her use language like that, either.

"The gutless b******!"

Mom phones the police and reports it as a break-in. She calls up a twenty-four-hour security company and gets them to come around and change the locks. When that's done, she pours herself a whisky and slumps down on the couch.

"We need a bigger TV!" she announces. "And we need cable!"

Then she remembers the wine bottles and falls apart again.

Will

When a girl like Vanessa says, "Let's go shopping for clothes," you have very few options. "I don't like shopping," "I don't need new clothes"—these are not options. The school year is almost over. The end-of-year party is on Saturday, and Vanessa is putting her foot down.

"I'm not taking you *anywhere* in that tracksuit," she says.

Vanessa is Versace, and I am her supermodel. She is Picasso, and I am her blank canvas. She is Coca-Cola, and I am her billboard.

The clothing department at T—— is understaffed.

With our arms full of clothing, we find an empty changing room. I begin trying things on, while Vanessa sits outside, passing me different garments under the door. I come out to do a catwalk, so Vanessa can tell me what she thinks.

"Nice in the butt!"

"Bit tight at the front, though."

"That's because they're girls' jeans."

"What!"

I am inside the changing room, getting into my next pair of pants, when the door suddenly opens and there is Vanessa, looking me up and down in my boxers. In my hurry to pull up my pants, I lose my balance and fall over.

"Sorry." She laughs. "I couldn't help myself."

In the end we both agree on a pair of fake Doc Martens, some baggy canvas pants, and a blue short-sleeved shirt. It's more than I can afford, but Vanessa has an idea.

"Do a swap," she says. "Leave your old clothes here and just walk out."

"I can't do that."

"Sure you can. That's a pretty fancy tracksuit, isn't it?"

"What about the security guard?"

Vanessa steps into the changing room. There isn't much room left after she closes the door. I feel her hand slip down the back of my pants as she pulls off the label. She does the same with the shirt and boots. There are no more labels, but the clothes still look new.

"No way!" I say. "They'll know."

"One more thing," she says.

Vanessa kneels down in front of me. She sticks out her tongue and licks both her open hands. I watch in helpless amazement as she rubs her wet palms down the front of my pants, making them look wrinkled and worn.

"How's that?" she says.

I am speechless.

My new clothes feel strange and slightly uncomfortable, but Vanessa reassures me I look "much better." Leaving my tracksuit and sneakers behind in the changing room, we walk out the main entrance. The security guard is too busy staring at Vanessa to even notice me.

Mia

"Really, Mia. You don't have to."

"But Mom, I *want* to!"

Cooking is fun. Shopping is fun. When the going gets tough, the tough go shopping. After the success of my Fettuccine Napoli, I am ready to do a Thai stir-fry!

The supermarket is chockablock with busy shoppers. The aisles are gridlocked with shopping carts, and the cash register lines are backed up for miles. *"Price check on register three. Price check on register three . . ."* It amazes me, how much food people buy. It amazes me how much time they spend standing in lines. If it wasn't for the magazines with their Hollywood parties and celebrity traumas, I'm sure we'd end up completely insane.

I am standing there reading about how Nicole Kidman is being brave when something catches my eye. I look up in horror as Will and Vanessa walk past together. They're not exactly hand in hand, but it's only a matter of time, I swear. Vanessa is smiling like a machete as they cut their way through the crowd. And Will is wearing new clothes!

Oh, Nicole! What are we going to do?

I come out of the supermarket, my cart stacked with tins of baby corn and bamboo shoots, packets of rice, and all the magazines and chocolate bars I have suddenly bought on impulse. I will go home to my little girl's bedroom and make myself into a pimply, fat reject.

Pushing my cart through the parking lot, I see Dad's four-wheel drive parked by the main entrance at the bottom of the sloping hill. A young woman is in the front seat, doing her lipstick in the rearview mirror, puckering up and practicing her smooches. I stand there, completely mesmerized. It's *her*!

T*** is in her early thirties. Her face is pleasant, but not pretty. Her hair is blond, but not natural. Her eyeliner is too obvious, and her earrings are a bit desperate. Why is she doing this, making herself look beautiful for a middle-aged man? Why is she stealing someone's husband, someone's father, my father! I hate her! I hate her ugly face and her red puckering lips. That is my dad's mirror. That is my dad's car. T*** is sitting in my mom's seat. It is because of *her* that my mom and dad don't love each other. It is because of *her* that my viola is broken. It is because of *her* that Will is with Vanessa.

I hate her and I want to slap her stupid puckering mouth!

As hard as I can, I give my shopping cart a push. With my fists clenched in furious revenge, I watch it hurtle toward Dad's car. It is too late to run and stop it. It is out of control and picking up speed. The castor wheels are wobbling furiously, but the cart stays right on course—a deadly missile, guided by hate.

T*** looks up just in time to see it coming. Her lips unpucker into comical disbelief. She sees me standing there with that terrible look on my face, and when I see how it shocks her, I suddenly feel ashamed. Together, with a kind of helpless dread, we watch the cart as it veers away just in time. It hits the gutter and falls with a loud crash, spilling food everywhere. Cars back up and toot their horns as Tina gets out of the car, and together we pick it all up. There is rice everywhere, as if someone just got married.

Will

The whiskers on my chin are getting darker and more prickly. Growing sideburns might be several years away, but a goatee beard is now a definite possibility. Taking extra-special care, I shave my cheeks, my neck, and under my jaw, trying to decide where the fluffy part ends and the goatee might start. A goatee would be good—I could stroke it to look like I was thinking. With a goatee, I could buy beer. I could look like I'd finished school.

After a few failed experiments I shave my chin and splash on some of Ken's Old Spice. The aftershave burns, but it helps stop shaving rash. I smell like a golfer, but the party is still three hours away—two hours and forty-five minutes, to be exact. I feel nervous, the way I usually feel before a big game of tennis, but it's not just the party I feel nervous about. It's what Ken might call "performance anxiety."

Vanessa said she was "*so much* looking forward to it." She said she would "wear something raunchy," just for me. "Raunchy"—I looked it up. It means either "vulgar and smutty," "openly sexual," or "untidy." I am pretty sure Vanessa won't be wearing anything untidy. I am pretty sure she is "so much looking forward" to more than just the party.

I imagine Vanessa in a skintight shiny black Catwoman suit laced up the sides, wearing black knee-high boots and a black cat mask. At the party she takes my hand and leads me off into a private room, with a tiger-skin rug and matching bedspread. Vanessa locks the door and tells me to lie down. She kneels beside me and strokes my shaved cheek with her dangerously long fingernails. She shows me which string to pull, the one that will undo all the laces of her cat suit from top to bottom. I take the string lightly between my fingers and slowly pull, as Vanessa removes her cat mask to reveal her true self. Except, suddenly, she isn't Vanessa anymore.

"Mia?"

"What sort of a dumb fantasy *is* this?" says Mia.

Mia

Normally, before a party, I check my wardrobe to see what my options are. For something as important as the end-of-year party, I might even go shopping for a new outfit. But because of everything that's been happening lately, I haven't been much in the mood.

To get ready for the party I take a shower and blow-dry my hair. (I'm not asking Mom to help iron it.) I get all my best clothes and lay them out on the bed—all my pants, tops, skirts, and dresses. One after the other I try them on, starting with the pants.

The 501s are too long—they need shortening. The red cotton pants are too short—somehow they've shrunk in the wash. The green denims are too loose around the waist. The stretch denims are too tight. The yellow pants are . . . yellow, what *was* I thinking? The black cords have lint on them, but so far they are my best bet.

The bluey green top is nice, but I've worn it too much lately. The greeny blue top makes me feel too fat. The pink sweater—best with a red bra—has a stain on the front. The Billabong top looks pretty cool, but the pants are Billabong, and I don't want to look like a walking ad campaign. The black tops aren't good with black pants—it's not a funeral. The white tops are too bright—I don't want to look like a waitress. The denim shirt is too "cowgirl," and you can't wear a cord shirt with cord pants, of course.

All my dresses are too light and summery, except for the ones that are too heavy and wintery. There are skirts, but skirts need tops, meaning the nightmare starts all over again. All my shoes are either too formal or too casual—there is nothing in between. The high heels are too high, impossible to dance in. The slip-ons are too loose and floppy.

I am in trouble. Even my jewelry is starting to look satanic.

When all else fails, I decide, make up your face.

I was never a big makeup girl, so there isn't much that can go wrong. A bit of lip gloss, some mascara, a touch of pink eye shadow, and I am done. In the mirror I see two rebel eyebrow hairs, hanging down in the most undesirable way. It takes three pairs of tweezers to get at them, and when I finally do, there is an ugly red blotch spreading halfway up my forehead. It's an emergency! I wash my face in cold water, then apply an ice pack. The red blotch turns to pink, then fades to a cold, numb white, so I pinch the skin and apply a hot facecloth to bring back the circulation.

I think about all those Hollywood stars in the glossy magazines—all the trouble they go to and how they complain about never being left alone. I think of Vanessa and what she might wear to the party. No matter what makeup or clothes I wear, compared to Vanessa, I will always look second best.

I am crazy to be putting myself through so much hell.

With a big blob of cleansing cream, I rub off all my makeup. Then, in a burst of fury, I throw all my clothes onto the floor and fall on my bed, crying.

I may as well wear a potato sack. I may as well go naked!

From the bottom drawer, I take out my shabby white tracksuit. It's pilled and smells of mothballs, but at least it still fits me. I dig out my old sneakers and two odd socks. I tie my hair back in a ponytail and put on my glasses, even though I don't really need them. I am going to the most important social event of my whole life, and I look like a total idiot.

It feels fantastic!

Will

"Dave! Have you brushed your teeth?"

"Yes, Will."

"Are you sure, Dave?"

"Sure, I'm sure, Will. You can check my toothbrush if you don't believe me."

"Did you wet your toothbrush, Dave, just to trick me?"

"You're not my boss, Will! You can't make me do something I don't want to do!"

"Do whatever you want, Dave. I don't care if your teeth fall out."

"If I brush my teeth, Will, can I come to the party?"

"No, Dave."

"Why not, Will?"

"Because it's late, Dave, and you're going to bed."

"Will Mia be there, Will?"

"Probably, Dave."

"Can we take Harriet out for a walk, Will?"

"I'll ask her, Dave."

"Please can I come to the party, Will?"

"The party is just for the kids in my class, Dave. You won't know anyone."

"I'll know Mia!"

"You can't come, Dave."

"You're mean, Will! You just don't want me to come because you're embarrassed about me! You don't want everyone to know your brother is in a wheelchair."

"I don't want everyone to know my brother is a pain in the ass!"

"I want you to stay home, Will! I want you to stay home and look after me!"

"I'm going to the party, Dave. And you're not coming."

"You don't care, Will! You don't care about our family!"

Mia

The party is in a garage, at the back of Yorick's house. There's a table of food and drinks, a few colored lights, and a sound system. Yorick's parents make a brief appearance to remind us that there is no alcohol allowed, then they wisely return to the house and leave us alone.

More important than *what* you wear to a party is *how* you wear it. If you turn up at a party with nipple chains and green spiky hair, it can go either way. People are either going to be impressed, or they're going to laugh at you. It all depends on your attitude. The only way to make the tracksuit work, I know, is to go with it and not to shy away. No apologies. No regrets. I'm wearing a white tracksuit, and I'm comfortable. What could be simpler than that?

"Hey, Mia! Cool outfit!"

"Bold fashion statement, girl!"

"It's like what New York rappers wear, only . . . white!"

"Actually," I say, "I'm wearing a sequined bikini underneath."

It is my fifteen minutes of fame. I am the center of attention. Everyone loves the tracksuit. It's like the best fancy-dress outfit, except this isn't a fancy-dress party. But then, fifteen minutes later, the novelty has worn off, and there I am, at the party, wearing only a tracksuit, after all.

Will

Vanessa buys the cans while I wait outside in the street. Vanessa won't need ID. In her silky new dress she looks twenty-one, at least. Through the window I see her talking to the guy across the counter. Why is Vanessa coming to this party when she could be sitting in a pub getting free rounds of drinks from executives in expensive suits? Why is she coming to the party with me?

Vanessa exits the liquor store with a wink, and we walk to the nearest bus stop. She pops the top of a can and takes a big long swig. Her mouth and lips almost kiss the can as she drinks, and her throat makes little gulping sounds as she swallows.

Vanessa passes the can to me, and I taste her lips as I drink from it. This is how kissing Vanessa would taste. Vanessa would kiss me like she swigs from a can. She would kiss me as if she were thirsty.

I am drinking from the can when suddenly Vanessa lies across the seat with her head in my lap! She closes her eyes and starts singing. It's a song I've never heard before, but the message is pretty obvious. All I need to do is lean down and kiss her. . . .

"Would you like another swig?" I say, instead.

Mia

Finally, they arrive. Vanessa does her big entrance in a dress that is elegant *and* braless, while Will tags along like a bodyguard. He is wearing new clothes and carrying some cans of bourbon and cola. By the way they're both walking, it looks as though they've already drunk some.

While Vanessa is basking in the spotlight, Will wanders over.

"What's the difference," he says, "between a viola and a lawn mower?"

He opens a can and offers it to me. I take a sip and feel it go straight to my head.

"A viola is sharper?" I say.

Will laughs. His breath smells of alcohol, and he's forgotten the punch line.

"You want another swig?" he says.

"I think you've had enough for both of us."

Will looks at me strangely. "Both of us," he slurs. "That's you and me, right?"

"What are you talking about?"

Will's face is so drunk and serious now, it is almost touching.

"I'm talking about you and me," he says. "I'm talking about us."

"And Vanessa," I say.

Will looks confused.

"Your date," I say. "Remember?"

Vanessa comes over. "Mia!" she says. "You make us all look so *overdressed*! What's that perfume you're wearing? It smells like mothballs."

"Mothballs, by Dior," I say.

Will laughs, and Vanessa smiles coldly.

"Let's go outside," she tells Will. "I'm dying for a smoke."

Will

Vanessa takes my hand and leads me through the party. She is my speedboat, and I am her water-skier. We brush past people, and she introduces me. "This is Will. . . . Say hi! Will." Vanessa has all the answers. She knows what to say. I am treading water when Vanessa throws me a rope. Hang on tight! She accelerates suddenly, and I'm up again, skimming across the smooth water. "Say hi! Will," she says, as we glide past the arm wrestlers. "This way," she says, as I sidestep Yorick, sticking out in front of me like a dead tree. Vanessa has an outboard motor. She's loud and fast and dangerous. She takes the corners sharp, and I swing out wide, holding on tight. Here comes the ski jump!

"At last!" she says, when we finally get outside. "Wasn't it *awful* in there?"

The ski rope goes slack. Vanessa stops to bum a cigarette from Rogers, the resident school player and name-dropper. "You look *amazing*!" says Rogers. "I *feel* good," says Vanessa. "I bet you do," says Rogers, looking her up and down. Rogers wants to take Vanessa's photograph, he says. He has his bedroom set up as a studio, he says, and his laundry as a darkroom. "We could do a shoot," he says. "We could put together a portfolio."

Rogers is reading Vanessa like a new-edition street directory, and he's headed straight for the Central Business District! Meanwhile, I am treading water again, only this time I'm out of my depth. The discarded ski rope tangles around my legs. I take another swig from my can as I feel myself going under. . . .

Mia

As Will disappears with Vanessa, the St. D. boys appear in the doorway, drinking beer and laughing loudly. They aren't wearing their school blazers, of course, but it's hard to not notice them. Do they know it's no alcohol? Do they know they are crashing?

Of course they do.

Bryce and his friends watch the crashers as they move into the room. The crashers are better dressed. They have beer, and they are offering it to some of the girls. Bryce and his friends are not happy.

The mood of the room changes abruptly. People stop dancing and move to the corners, leaving the crashers alone in the middle. One of them shakes up his beer, and it sprays the roof when he opens it. Someone belches loudly, and the others laugh. The crashers see the table of food and begin to help themselves.

Then in walks Yorick.

"Excuse me," he tells the crashers. "You're not supposed to be here."

The crashers look at Yorick. If they weren't standing in a room full of people who were thinking the same thing, they might not be so polite.

"It is a party, isn't it?" says one of them, with his mouth full.

"In fact," says Yorick, "it's an end-of-year party for our school. The problem is, you don't go to our school, do you?"

Yorick would make a great lawyer. He makes it sound

like a genuine question, requiring a genuine answer. But the subtlety is lost on the crashers.

"Are you telling us to leave?" they say.

Yorick looks uncertain, as if he has only just seen the trouble he is getting himself into. Luckily, Bryce decides to step forward.

"It's probably a good idea, don't you think?"

The crashers have no alternative. They take their cans and leave. Bryce and his friends move into the middle, and someone turns up the music.

Will

According to *The Encyclopedia of Tennis*, a match may be terminated in any of the following ways: (1) When it's a "walkover"—a game that never began, awarded to the victor when the loser concedes defeat; (2) when a player quits due to inability or injury; (3) when you are disqualified for violating the rules of conduct. (4) When your opponent promises photographs for a modeling portfolio. (5) When cigarettes are borrowed and the borrower is overheard to say "I will pay you back later," probably with interest. (6) When your opponent's flirting turns into dirty dancing. (7) When the retiring player sees the girl he *really* likes—the girl he has treated badly and ruined his chances with—smiling in sympathy from across the crowded room. (8) When a player decides that YES! now is the time to make amends for all his past mistakes, and YES! he will finally bite the bullet and say what *must be said* to this girl of his dreams, whatever that is. (9) When the player takes a deep breath, trusting that *how he feels* about this girl will be enough to get him by, *how he feels* will provide all the answers, even despite "Once a choker, always a choker." (10) When the player realizes he has had too much to drink and suddenly feels like throwing up. . . .

Mia

The dance floor starts to clear. People leave the garage and start moving down the driveway. There is something going on. The crashers are up to something. . . .

Out in the street, a crowd gathers round to watch what is happening. The crashers are there in the middle, but it is hard to make out what they are doing. Some of the girls look horrified. Some of the boys are smiling. Yorick is in there with the crashers, stretched like a sagging hammock, being held by his arms and legs. His pants are down around his ankles, and his body is limp. It's a horrible sight, but the worst thing is the look on Yorick's face. He isn't struggling or shouting for help. Instead, his eyes have that faraway look, as if he's trying to pretend it isn't happening.

"Nature strip!" cheers one of the crashers.

"Pull his underwear down!" another agrees.

"Oh, no!" laughs Vanessa. "I can't bear to watch!"

But where is Will?

Vanessa stays where she is, and so does everyone else. The show isn't over yet. Bryce is comforting a girl in his arms. Someone makes a joke and all the boys laugh. Some girls are standing at a distance. Their faces say they disapprove, but they also look curious.

Yorick's body hangs limply like a piece of meat. His skin is white with goose bumps, and his boxers are white, too. The crashers have the crowd on their side now. They start swinging Yorick slowly from side to side, as the crowd begins to chant:

"Yor-ick! . . . Where's-his-prick! . . . Yor-ick! . . . Where's-his-prick!"

Like a lost boat on a stormy sea, Yorick's body lurches and sways as the crashers swing him higher. He closes his eyes, and his mouth twists in fear. The people at the back push forward for a better view. Their faces shine with excitement and disgust and relief. Everyone has the same look in their eyes: *I'm glad it's not me.*

"Yor-ick! . . . Where's-his-prick! . . . Yor-ick! . . . Where's-his-prick!"

I don't understand. Is it just harmless fun or has everyone gone insane? Am I the only one who can see what is happening?

I wish Will were here.

Will

A toilet bowl is the worst place in the world to throw up in: (a) it stinks, (b) it's too small, (c) it's too low to the ground, (d) you have to kneel down to make sure you don't miss, meaning that it stinks even more, (e) you have to stick your head right in there, meaning that your head is now *inside* a toilet, where countless humans have sat over the years depositing countless deposits that you don't want to think about, and (f) why do I list everything all the time, anyway?

The only good thing about toilets is, they make you want to throw up.

When I finally emerge from the toilet, the garage is empty. Everyone is out in the street. I'm walking down the driveway, feeling sober, but completely disgusting, when I hear someone scream: "STOP IT, YOU ANIMALS!"

Mia is there in the middle of the crowd. She and one of the crashers are wrestling over something—it looks like a leg. As I push people aside and make my way toward them, I see Yorick with his pants down, wriggling and squirming as someone pours cold beer onto his bare white skin. I don't need to see anything else.

I go straight for the prick with the beer can. I grab him in a headlock and pull him to the ground. In a flash, the other boys drop Yorick to help their friend. One tries to drag me off him, while another lands a punch on the side of my head. Instantly, Bryce and Co. step out of the crowd to help me, and a full-scale brawl erupts.

Mia

It's as if someone flicked a lighted match onto a pool of gasoline. Everywhere, guys are throwing punches and rolling around on the grass, elbowing and head-butting, kicking and scratching, shouting obscenities and making stupid threats. Someone's head is bleeding. Someone else has lost a tooth. Girls are screaming for them to stop, but no one hears them. Suddenly, even the nicest guy has turned into a desperate, ugly monster. And in the midst of it all, Yorick is sitting there, stunned and abandoned, with his beer-soaked pants down around his ankles.

The fighting and yelling continues—it just goes on and on. I am standing alone, surrounded by violence, but instead of feeling frightened, I begin to feel calm. As the fight spins out of control all around me, the noise and confusion slow to a blur, and I almost feel invisible.

Will is there, in among it all. I try to move toward him, but someone blocks my way. Then a guy with a beer can hits him on the back of the head, and Will falls to the ground, unconscious.

Will

When I open my eyes, it feels like I've died and gone to heaven. Above me there are clusters of stars, trailing meteors, and planets spinning in elliptical orbits. There are exploding supernovas, spiraling galaxies, and a great big photograph of Albert Einstein.

"Where am I?"

Mia holds my hand and squeezes it gently. Her face is more beautiful than the sun and more serious than

Einstein. "You're in Yorick's bedroom," she says.

"Is Yorick okay?"

Mia looks relieved. "He's on the Internet," she says, "e-mailing his invisible friends about it. How about you? Are you okay?"

"I think so. What happened?"

Mia lets go of my hand. "You were out cold," she says. "Everyone was worried sick. There's a doctor on the way."

Yorick's bed smells of toast and peanut butter. I try sitting up, but it's not worth the effort. I lie back down, looking up at the universe. I want to hold Mia's hand again to stop myself floating away.

Mia frowns. "Are you sure you're okay?"

"Pretty sure."

"I hope so," says Mia. "It's our concert tomorrow night, and I'd really like you to come."

I try so hard not to smile, I end up frowning.

"Only if you want to," Mia adds.

The doctor arrives. He checks my head for cuts and bruises, while Mia stands in the doorway watching. He takes my pulse and shines a pencil light in each eye.

"Mild concussion," he diagnoses. "Stay warm, take Tylenol, and get some rest."

The doctor wants to know all about what has happened and how I feel. He explains how the skull protects the cerebrum, how the brain itself feels no pain, and how quick it is to recover from most injuries. The doctor is very friendly. He seems in no hurry to leave, and when Mia brings him a cup of tea, he even looks grateful.

"Thanks for coming," she says. "I'm sorry I dragged you out of bed."

"Think nothing of it," he says.

"I was wondering," she says, "if you could give Will a lift home."

"With pleasure," he says.

Mia smiles. "Thanks, Dad," she says.

Mia

Will and I sit in the backseat as my father drives him home. My father is still doing his doctor/patient thing—being very charming and informative—but I get the feeling Will isn't listening. He looks out the window, then turns and smiles at me, then looks away again. I don't know what it is about the backseat, but suddenly I'm very conscious of being there in the darkness, with nothing but space between us and only seat belts to restrain us.

Along with everything else, of course.

Will

Lyn and Ken are waiting at the front gate. They help me out of the car, thank Mia and Dr. Foley, then escort me back into the house. Lyn makes a cup of hot chocolate while Ken makes me comfortable on the couch, then they insist on hearing the whole story.

"There's not much to it," I say. "It was over in a flash."

"You were brave to step in like that," Ken says.

"You could have been seriously hurt," says Lyn.

"I was helping a friend," I say.

Ken and Lyn and I sit up, talking about tennis, and how fame and happiness don't necessarily go together. We talk about how being fifteen is weird because you're not a child anymore, but you're not an adult either. We talk about how it's important to think about the future, but more important to take each day as it comes. It sounds like a conversation where the adults do most of the talking, but for most of the time Ken and Lyn just sit there, holding hands and listening. It's strange when you suddenly realize that your parents value your opinion, but even stranger when you see they're actually proud of you!

The only time Lyn and Ken look worried is when I tell them about Dave wanting to come to the party.

"He thinks you don't care about him," says Lyn.

"He feels as if you're grown-up but he's still a baby," says Ken.

"Tomorrow," I say. "We'll go into town."

I get up and say good night, then wander off down the hall to bed. Dave's bedroom is opposite mine, and for the first time his door is shut.

Mia

I lie in my bed, imagining a rain forest. There are leafy ferns and jungle vines, exotic birds and monkeys swinging from the trees. My bedroom is a tree house, high up in the canopy where no one can reach me and no one else can see. Tomorrow Will is coming to the concert—he's coming to hear me play! The rain forest is alive with noise. The screeches of birds and the howls of monkeys fill the warm, moist air. Far below me on the forest floor, there are poisonous frogs, crawling insects, and giant pythons. Will is coming to the concert, and after the concert, what then? My rain forest is a wild place where no one has ever been before. It's a Garden of Eden—a place where a girl can be who she wants to be. All I need to do is grab a vine and swing down into it.

Six

Will

At eleven o'clock the next morning, Lyn pokes her head around my bedroom door.

"How are you feeling?" she asks.

"Pretty ordinary."

"Ken and I are going shopping. Can you look after Dave?"

"Sure."

I don't know if it's a hangover or the bump on my head or a combination, but my brain feels like an old computer that's been taken to the tip—busted and rusted beyond repair. I gather up the energy to get myself out of bed. I take a shower, fix myself a flotilla of Mini-Wheats, then sit back to watch the Saturday-morning cartoons. When Duck Dodgers gets disintegrated, I know exactly how he feels.

I think about Mia inviting me to the concert and whether or not it's a date. After all, we won't be sitting together. We may not even get a chance to speak. But the fact is, Mia asked me to come, so headache or no headache, I'll be there.

When the cartoons finish, it's midday, and still there's no sign of Dave.

I knock quietly on his bedroom door, but there's no answer.

"Dave?" When I turn the handle and try to open the door, it's jammed.

"Dave? Are you in there?"

"Go away, Will!"

"Are you still mad at me?"

"I'm not talking to you, Will. You can't make me."

"I'm supposed to be looking after you, Dave. I thought we could go and see Mia. We could take Harriet for a walk, if you want to."

It's an excellent offer—easily good enough, I would have thought, to lure Dave out of his room.

"You can't make me, Will."

"Okay, Dave," I say. "You wait here while I go and get Harriet."

Mia

I slop on the wallpaper remover, and like magic, the wallpaper peels away in long thin strips. The walls beneath are smooth and bare—as vulnerable as trees that have lost their bark. Should I paint them green, to go with the indoor plants and ferns? Or should I paint bright butterflies, dancing in the sunlight?

The doorbell rings, and Mom answers it. I hear footsteps coming down the hall, and when I look up, *there he is*, inside my house! Standing in my doorway, looking into my unfinished bedroom! Staring at my stripped walls before they're even ready!

"Will!"

Will nods at the borrowed viola on my bed.

"Shouldn't you be practicing for the concert tonight?" he says.

"Are you still coming?"

"Of course I'm still coming."

"You don't have to, if you don't want to."

Will grins. "I'll be there, even if I have to come on crutches."

"Even if I'm not the star of the show?"

"Even if they don't give out trophies," he says.

"What are you doing here, anyway?" I say. "Shouldn't you be at home, resting?"

Will lowers his head to show me how the swelling has gone down. I am seriously tempted to run my fingers through his hair. I don't, of course.

"Actually—" he says. "Can I borrow Harriet?"

Will

Dogs are smart. There's no doubt about it. No animal has adapted better to a world dominated by humans. Instead of being put on the menu or hunted to extinction, dogs have been able to work out what people want. They know how to sit up and beg for food, how to bark at strangers or fetch a stick, while at the same time looking cute enough for people to think that their dog is actually their friend. But a dog is a dog. It's an animal, trying to survive. It does what it can to get a bowl of meat and a safe place to sleep. I never wanted one as a pet, and I'm not about to be suddenly swept away by a cute little beagle.

After walking a couple of blocks together, Harriet and I have an understanding. We walk fast, with Harriet a step ahead and to the side. Yes, Harriet is excited to be out on the leash. No, we don't stop to smell the doggy poo or to annoy the barking dogs behind fences. Harriet walks with her head down and tail up, turning now and then to give me a reassuring glance: *I'm Harriet, the sniffer dog,* she says, *off on another great adventure.*

"You don't fool me, Harriet. But if you can get Dave out of his bedroom, I'll buy you a nice big bone."

Not a problem, says Harriet, with her doggy smile.

When we get home, I knock loudly on Dave's door, but he doesn't answer.

"Dave! Come and see who's here!"

Harriet barks in excitement, but there is still no answer. This time, when I try the door, it opens. But the room is empty and on the bed there's a note in Dave's big, neat handwriting:

I have RUN AWAY! it says. *Don't try to find me. I am NEVER coming back!*

Mia

The wallpaper is gone. I have pulled down the curtains. The bedspread is packed away, ready for the Salvation Army. Next on my list is the hideous chandelier.

I get a stepladder from the laundry and climb up it for a closer look. If it is possible to unscrew the crystal monstrosity, I will be happy enough with just a lightbulb for now (green bulb? forty-watt?). I am up on the stepladder, deciding how *not* to electrocute myself, when there's another knock at the front door.

"I'll get it, Mom!" I call out, assuming it must be Will, returning Harriet after her walk. I take off my glasses and neaten my hair, but when I open the door, I get a shock.

"Dad?"

Last night, as a doctor, my father was comfortable and relaxed. Now, as a father, he looks nervous and uncertain. When I go to kiss him, he doesn't know whether to hug me or not. I don't know if Mom wants me to invite him in or not. I don't think I want him to see my room in such a mess, either.

"It's the big day!" he says.

"Yep." I nod. "The big day."

"I'm looking forward to it," he says.

"Me, too."

"I got you something," he says.

"You didn't have to."

My father goes to his car and comes back with my present. It's in a long, rectangular box, wrapped up in plain brown paper. The card simply says: *Sorry, love Dad.*

I sit down on the doorstep and fumble with the wrapping paper, while my father watches nervously. Inside the box is a beautiful new viola.

Will

"You're a bloodhound, Harriet! That's what bloodhounds do—they pick up the scent and run with it. They hunt foxes and rabbits. They catch drug smugglers. They track down escaped prisoners. Now, help me find Dave!"

Harriet sniffs at Dave's T-shirt then leaps into action. She tears down the hallway and disappears under the kitchen table, looking for food scraps.

I knew it was a dumb idea.

Dave has run away. He might be just around the corner, or he might be on the train heading cross-country. Surely, because of his wheelchair, he can't have gone too far. How can someone run away from home when they can't even walk?

Mia

Mom invites Dad in, and together they watch me tune my new viola and play a few arpeggios. My new viola is *splendido e magnifico!* The wood is darker than the old viola, with a finer, less distinctive grain. The bridge is cut differently, and the f-holes are longer, but the feel of the neck and the tone of the two instruments are remarkably similar. My dad has gone to a lot of trouble in choosing it.

I close my eyes and pretend I am playing my old instrument. I pretend that nothing bad has happened— that my mom and dad still love each other, and that the three of us are a normal, happy family. I play the arpeggios with more feeling, and the tone of the instrument changes, becoming richer and more resonant. I realize, with tears streaming down my cheeks, that no two violas can ever be the same.

Will

Harriet's nose is a heavy-duty industrial vacuum cleaner—a super-sniffer, sucking up smells, searching for clues. The first place we look is the tennis court. It's the Saturday lessons, and while I ask around, Harriet entertains the children with "Sit" and "Lie down." By the time I am done, a tennis ball has been mauled, a toddler is crying, and a four-year-old is throwing a tantrum: "*I want a dog, Mommy! I* WANT *one!*" There has been no sign of Dave, though, so with no time to waste, we leave to continue our search. Harriet has no idea where we are going, but she's dragging me there anyway.

At the shopping center there is a sign on the automatic glass door. It shows an outline of a dog's body inside a red circle with a red diagonal line crossing it out. It might mean No Dogs, but it doesn't actually say so. And the more I look at the dog in the picture, the less it looks like Harriet. Some breeds of dog are obviously banned from the shopping center, but surely not tracker dogs here on urgent business.

Harriet and I sneak into SportsWorld and begin sniffing around for traces of Dave. We snoop around swimwear and creep through cricket. We slink past skiing and tiptoe through tennis. There are rackets on special, so surely Dave must be here, hiding in a changing room or eyeing a new pair of sneakers. SportsWorld is a big, busy store, but when Harriet starts making new friends, it's not long before we're noticed by the staff.

"Excuse me," says the girl. "Your dog is not allowed in here."

"She's not my dog," I say, hoping to buy some time.

"I'll have to get someone," she says.

The girl gets the section manager, the section manager gets the store manager, then the store manager gets the security guard. By the time the guard arrives, I have staked out the entire store, and Harriet is tearing around the Astroturf with a gang of squealing children.

"Let's go, Harriet. We're done here."

Outside the sports store, the food court is thundering with noise as people clatter their cutlery and slurp their cappuccinos. Out of desperation, I buy a $2 pair of sunglasses, hoping that people will think Harriet is my seeing-eye dog. The trouble is, seeing-eye dogs are known to stay cool in a tense situation, whereas Harriet is a dead giveaway—jumping up on tables, trying to lick kids' ice creams. There are too many different smells here for an innocent young bloodhound. Harriet's nose is in danger of being overloaded. She could rupture her sinuses or blow a nose gasket.

Instead, I tie her up outside the door and wander among the tables, searching without much hope for a sign of my runaway brother. How ridiculous am I, to be taking Dave's note so seriously? But time is slipping away, and I am starting to panic now. What if Dave really means it? What if he *really has* run away? Dave might have even *made plans*—a refuge for the disabled, a motorized wheelchair, a getaway van with a ramp up the back. Or worse, Dave might be in trouble. He might have done something stupid.

When I return, Harriet has wound her leash around the pole until she can't move her head. As a prisoner of her own stupidity, she is paying the price—a boy and his sister are mercilessly tickling her tummy, and Harriet's hind leg is scratching the air in ecstasy.

I unwind her leash, and we're away again, with Harriet relentlessly dragging me on.

At the swimming pool she makes her grand entrance, barking madly at the startled swimmers and wanting to leap into the water to join them. Surely Dave will be here, arguing with the lifeguards or wrestling with the vending machine? As I survey the lap swimmers, the rowdy kids doing cannonballs, and the soakers in the spa, I can hardly bear to look. At any moment I expect to see Dave, floating lifelessly in the water.

But no, he's not here, which means he's somewhere else. But where?

I am running out of possibilities.

The park, of course! Of course, Dave is in the park—doing his chin-ups, proving to himself, yet again, that he's stronger than his big brother. The park is the place I should have looked first. Dave isn't running away. He's in the park, waiting patiently to take Harriet for a walk.

The park seems like a long, long way from the pool. It's a sunny afternoon, and by the time Harriet and I get there, we are both panting loudly and soaked in sweat. The park is deserted. There is nothing but trees and grass in every direction. Out of desperation, I let Harriet off the leash, and she runs away, spurred on by some unknown excitement. I follow her at a distance, doing my best to keep up as she speeds toward the chin-up bars, barking with excitement. There, on the ground, I see something that lifts my hopes like a wave, then smashes them against the rocks.

It is Dave's empty wheelchair, collapsed and lying on its side.

Mia

"Should we call the police?" Mom asks, on the way to rehearsal.

"Definitely not!"

"What about Harriet? What if something has gone wrong?"

"Will is probably . . . caught up in something," I say, trying to sound convinced.

"Is he coming to the concert? Does he know when it starts?"

"He knows. . . . He's coming."

"Well, I hope he's not late. Remember, he's already let you down once."

"He won't be late, Mom. . . . He'd better not be."

Will

Dave has disappeared into thin air. Dave has evaporated. He has been abducted, assassinated, sold into slavery, murdered. Harriet is barking up a tree, but it's the wrong tree. There is no sign of Dave in any direction.

"Dave!" I shout. "Where are you?"

No answer. Not even an echo.

Harriet suctions the folded wheelchair for clues, then suddenly takes off across the grass in the direction of the lake. There's a big clump of reeds growing by the water's edge. Maybe Dave has crawled in there or *been dragged in there* by some mutant urban THING! Harriet is almost to the reeds when she hears another dog barking. From across the park, a mongrel comes running—a big ugly bruiser of a dog without a collar. Harriet stops. With her tail in the air she turns to face the new dog, who wastes no time in sniffing her out. But before Harriet has time to return the compliment, the brute is snarling. Harriet's tail drops. She yelps and tries to run, but the heavyweight mongrel grabs her by the throat and starts to shake her violently, trying to break her neck.

"GET AWAY!"

I pick up a stick and run toward them. When the mongrel sees me coming, it releases Harriet and bares its teeth. Instead of turning to run, it snaps its jaws again and—like Iron Mike Tyson—bites off a piece of Harriet's ear. Only after I hit it hard across its back and kick it does it finally run away.

Harriet is instantly on her feet, barking excitedly, with blood streaming from her mauled ear. From a tree beside the lake, I hear a wild thrashing of leaves. I look up and see Dave, half-falling, half-climbing down from way up high. A twig snaps, and I watch in horror as he topples head over heels, clears the lowest branch, and lands, somehow, on his feet! For what seems like forever, he stands in that miraculous position, screaming at the fleeing mongrel, before finally sinking to his knees.

"Dave!"

"Call an ambulance, Will! We've got to get Harriet to the hospital!"

Mia

I show Ms. Stanway my new viola while the orchestra is setting up on the stage. Ms. S. inspects it briefly, plays a few bars, and tells me I am a lucky girl. The musicians are tuning their instruments, playing their scales, and running through their different parts. There is no sound on earth so chaotic yet so full of expectation as an orchestra tuning. Ms. S. runs through her reminder notes, then she's in a snit about how we will take our bows and in what order, who will carry their instruments and who will leave them behind. In the time remaining, we play the Vivaldi—all twelve movements—stopping only once, when the woodwinds launch in two bars early. I play my parts without a mistake, but even on my new viola it is hard to play with passion. My eyes follow the notes without reading them, and my fingers go through the motions. Whenever anyone arrives or leaves the hall, I look up, hoping to see Will.

Will

Dave and I sit in the waiting room while behind the white door, the vet stitches Harriet's ear. I have never seen Dave so worried. He wriggles and fidgets and keeps asking questions.

"Will Harriet have a general anesthetic, Will, or just a local?"

"I don't know, Dave."

"Will it hurt, Will? Will she be scared?"

"She's a brave little dog, Dave."

"Will she be okay, Will? Will she still be able to hear?"

"I'm sure she'll be fine, Dave."

"Will you miss the concert? Will Mia be mad at you?"

"I hope not, Dave."

"It wasn't our fault, Will. It was that other dog. Why was it so angry, Will?"

"Some dogs are bred to fight, Dave."

"Why do people *have* dogs like that, Will?"

"Some people are like their dogs, Dave. They're bred to fight."

"But we weren't scared of it, were we, Will?"

"I was a bit scared, Dave."

"Me too, Will."

"You didn't look scared, Dave. You looked angry."

"Dogs know it when you're scared, don't they, Will? They can smell fear."

"Everyone can smell it, Dave."

"Is that why you lost the tennis match, Will?"

"I don't know, Dave. Maybe."

"But you're not a choker, Will. You weren't scared of those boys at the party."

"I was a bit scared, Dave."

"Did you ever feel like running away, Will?"

"I think everyone feels like running away sometimes, Dave."

"It would be pretty stupid if everyone ran away, Will. Where would they all go?"

"How did you get up that tree, Dave?"

"I climbed, of course."

"But how did you get there without your wheelchair?"

Dave grins. "What do you think I am, Will? Disabled?"

Mia

Boys are unreliable. They are fundamentally, genetically, and *primordially* unreliable. They will do anything to try and meet you, but then they can't talk. They will invite you to the tennis matches, even though they can't actually *be* there. They will trample your flowers. They will treat you like cattle. They will sleaze around with your ex-best friend. They will promise to come to the most important event in your life, but instead they will steal your dog and never come back. Will Holland is unreliable—he cannot be relied on. If this was a tennis match; if I was an athlete, instead of a musician; if there were any gold medals to be won or toe-sucking to be had, I'm sure things would be different.

Slowly but steadily, the clock ticks down to starting time. The doors open, and people begin to stream in. They take their seats and start reading their programs—all the moms and dads and brothers and sisters and grannies and grand-pas and aunties and uncles, come to see the concert, come to be reliable. Mom and Dad arrive together, but not together, if you know what I mean. I give Mom a hopeful look, and she shakes her head grimly. No Harriet. No Will. Nothing to rely on.

The lights of the house go down, and Ms. Stanway walks onto the stage. She welcomes the audience and tells them about the composer.

"Antonio Vivaldi was born in Venice in 1678. A prolific composer and a virtuoso violinist, he was rich at the height of his fame but died in poverty. Of the 500 concertos he wrote, the most popular were four known as *Le Quattro Stagioni—The Four Seasons*."

The audience applauds as Ms. S. takes up her baton and turns to face the orchestra. We raise our instruments, and with a nod from Ms. S., we're away! Allegro—the first move-ment of *Spring*. It's the catchy, melodic, swingy, *springy* movement that everyone instantly recognizes and the orchestra knows by heart. There are a few tricky bits where the violins spin and weave like butterflies, then a fast bit for the strings, which we play almost perfectly. Ms. S. is smiling. All her hard work is paying off.

When the first movement ends, there's a brief pause before the second—*Largo e pianissimo sempre*. As the players turn the pages of their sheet music, preparing to start, there's a sound as explosive as gunshots, coming from the back of the hall.

Someone is clapping!

Will

Dave and I sneak in the door as the orchestra is starting. There are no empty seats. If Dave hadn't been in a wheelchair, we might not have been let in. We move to the back corner without being noticed, but when Dave starts clapping at the end of the first movement, people turn around in disgust. When they see who he is, their angry stares change to amusement, which in my book is even worse. Instead of telling Dave to stop clapping, I join in.

The second movement of *Spring* is a quiet, gentle number. It's impossible to say for sure what the music is all about, but because it's called *Spring*, I imagine a garden. The sun is shining, and bees are buzzing all around between the bright colored flowers. One bee is going about his business when it notices a particular flower. The more the bee looks at this flower, the more and more beautiful it seems. In the third movement the tempo picks up, and the bee starts to go a bit crazy. It buzzes around and around the flower, but doesn't have the nerve to land. In the end the bee returns to the hive, sad and honeyless.

When *Summer* comes, everything slows right down. The orchestra has a siesta while the first violinist kills a few blowflies, turns on the fan, and grabs a cool drink from the fridge. In the second movement he puts his feet up and watches baseball, then in the third everyone piles into the car and heads off to the beach. The sky is blue, and off in the distance two white yachts are racing across the sparkling water. It's hard to tell if they're having fun or desperately trying to outrun each other. When they get to the floating buoy, one turns around while the other keeps on going.

Autumn starts with a bang. It's as if there's a big game of soccer between two old rivals. After getting off to a good start, the game begins to get messy. Someone kicks the ball out of the stadium, then the players start fighting and the umpire accidentally gets flattened. The second movement is slow, like falling leaves. The soccer game has been abandoned, and now everyone is out in the park, helping to rake up the leaves. They make a pile as big as a bonfire, then in the third movement, someone lights a match and the whole thing goes up in smoke.

When *Winter* comes, the scene shifts to Antarctica. There are mountains of ice and glaciers breaking up into icebergs. In the howling wind, weary explorers are trudging

knee-deep through the endless snow. In the second movement one of the explorers falls down a crack and has to be
thrown a rope. It's a tense situation, but they finally get him
out, unharmed. By the third and final movement they're all
back at base camp, enjoying a cup of hot chocolate. It's a bit
of an anticlimax, really.

Suddenly everyone in the audience is on his or her feet,
applauding loudly. For the entire concert the only noise
between movements has been old people coughing, babies
crying, or Dave asking me if he can clap yet.

"Go for it, Dave!" I say.

The two of us let rip, stomping and whistling until
Ms. Stanway walks back on stage. The audience sits down
as the orchestra prepares to play an encore.

The encore they choose is *Spring*, so that the concert
ends as it started, and the seasons continue in an unbroken
cycle. Just when you think things are all over, they're starting
up again.

I look up at Mia, and she sees me. I give her a big thumbs-
up, to say that Harriet is fine, and she smiles and mouths
the words "Thank you," as if she can guess what we have
been through.

It's spring, all over again.

Mia

After the show there's coffee and cake out in the hall. I
talk to Mom and Dad, then I talk to someone else's mom

and dad, then someone else's grandma and grandpa. Everyone says what a wonderful concert it was and how beautifully we played. It doesn't matter that I've never seen these people before and will probably never see them again. It feels like one big happy family.

Will and his brother are there in the corner, and finally I get a chance to speak to them. But before Will can say anything, Dave is pumping my arm and raving loudly:

"It was fantastic, but we almost didn't make it! Poor Harriet! But she's okay, don't worry. I loved *The Four Seasons*, especially the parts when everyone played at the same time. It was so loud! Are you having another concert, because if you are I want to come. Do you have a CD? Where can I buy it? Tell her that joke, Will—the one about the viola and the trampoline!"

I turn to Will. "What happened to Harriet?"

"She's back at our place," he says. "She was helping me find Dave."

Will

Mia wants to see Harriet. Her mom says it's okay, so she and Dave and I walk home together. Dave is lapping up Mia's attention. He tells her in gory detail all about Harriet's fight, and how he jumped out of a tree to save her.

"I've decided I don't want to run away from home," he says. "I want to play in an orchestra. I want to learn an instrument like that black one with all the knobs and the silver blower on the end. Will says it's called a baboon!"

Harriet is in our laundry room, curled up on an old blanket. She's sedated and bandaged but happy to see us. Mia has tears in her eyes as she kneels down beside the little beagle to give her a loving hug.

"You were so brave, girl. There are some nasty dogs out there."

Harriet is not to be moved, so Mia promises to come back in the morning. When I offer to walk her home, Dave is already halfway out the door.

"What about me, Will? Can I come, too? What do you think, Mia? Would that be okay?"

Mia takes Dave's hand, which shuts him up better than a roll of masking tape.

"Another time, Dave," she says. "Will and I need to talk."

Mia

It's a warm, misty night. Will and I walk slowly along the main road, looking in the shop windows, reading the price tags, feeling the tiny droplets on our skin, and hearing the occasional *swish* of a passing car. We don't need to talk about the concert. We don't need to talk about music or sports. We don't need to talk about Harriet or Dave. We don't need to talk about our parents or our friends, about the past or the future. We don't need to talk about feelings or facts, about being reliable or redecorating our bedrooms. It's warm and misty, with the feeling of invisible raindrops in the soft night air. Will and I are happy just walking. We don't need to talk. . . .

Will

Talk? What is there to talk about? *Don't forget V!* Is Mia still upset about Vanessa? Or has she fallen in love with the first violinist? (*V* for *Virtuoso?*) If Mia wants to talk, then why isn't she talking? Does she expect me to launch into an apology when I didn't even kiss Vanessa? Or is she waiting to break the news gently about her and the talented Mr. V? Should I say something? Should I break the ice? Should I apologize one more time about Harriet? Should I tell her how beautiful she looked up on the stage?

Mia and I walk on in silence up the main road. Up ahead of us the hands on the clock tower are covering the twelve. Either it's midnight, or the clock is broken. Mia stops walking and turns to face me. This is it—the big *V*—the thing she wants to talk about.

"Look up in the sky," she says.

Mia looks like Cinderella, but I think I'm about to get hit by a falling pumpkin.

Mia

I ask Will, "What do you see up there?"

He looks uncertain. "Clouds?"

"Do you ever think about raindrops?"

"Raindrops?"

"Did you ever think about what happens when two raindrops fall on the top of a mountain? One raindrop rolls down one side of the mountain, then into a stream, then a river, before it gets swept away into the sea. But the other raindrop runs off in a different direction, down into a different river, then off into a different ocean, maybe. The two raindrops started off so close but then ended up so far away."

"Maybe one day," says Will, choosing his words carefully, "they might meet again, in the clouds."

"Is that possible, do you think?"

"I'm sure it is."

Will

There is no pumpkin! There is no V! Mia is a modern-day Cinderella who doesn't care what time it is, A.M or P.M. She doesn't want to fight with me. She just wants to talk about the weather!

Mia and I leave the main road and walk through empty suburban streets with their parked cars and leafy trees, their picket fences and immaculate gardens. It feels like just the two of us now, while the rest of the world is asleep.

"What do you throw away when you need it," she says, "and pick up when you don't need it?"

"I give up. What?"

"It's a riddle," she says. "I'm not *telling* you. You have to work it out."

"What do you throw away when you need it—"

"—and pick up when you don't need it?"

"A light switch?"

"Wrong!"

"Chewing gum?"

"No."

"You're not going to tell me, are you?"

"Sorry."

"But I might never guess. I might go to my grave without knowing the answer."

"That would be sad."

"Secrets?"

"Incorrect."

"Time?"

"Hmm . . . No."

"A friend?"

"I hope not."

"A boomerang? A yo-yo?"

"No . . . and no."

"You're enjoying this, aren't you?"

Mia

"Underpants?"

"No."

"Odd socks?"

"No."

"DNA?"

"No."

"M&Ms?"

"No."

"Astronauts?"

"No."

"Eskimos?"

"You're not really trying anymore, are you?"

Will and I have come to a crossroads. All the streets look the same—north, south, east, and west. There is a traffic circle like a grassy green island with a big leafy tree in the center. We sit down like castaways, feeling stranded and invisible behind a curtain of mist. It is after midnight, but instead of feeling tired, I am almost dizzy with excitement. It doesn't feel late anymore, it feels early.

"Can you give me a clue?" says Will.

"I feel as if we're floating," I say.

"Floating?" Will thinks for a while. "A life buoy?"

"A life buoy gets thrown *at* you, doesn't it?"

"I've got it!" he says, suddenly.

"What is it?" I say. "What do you throw away when you need it and pick up when you don't need it?"

"An anchor!" he says.

"Yes!" I say, holding out my hand.

Will takes my hand and gently squeezes it.

"You're my anchor," he says, softly.

Will

Love is an anchor—it stops you from drifting away. Love is sticking up for your friends and family, or even your pets. Love is being brave and saying what you feel. Love is making music or playing tennis; it's doing what you want to do. Love is holding on and not letting go.

Mia

Will's hand feels soft and warm in mine, but also strong and determined. I feel his grip tighten as I gently pull toward him . . .

Will

. . . and we . . .

Mia

. . . kiss!

Seven

Will

One month later, my elbow is still pretty screwed up. Playing tennis is out—along with directing traffic and cooking with a wok—so Ken has given up trying to make me into a star. Instead, he and I are training Dave to be the star. Go, Dave!

Dave loves the attention, of course, but his favorite thing is walking Harriet. Dave is crazy about Harriet, and Harriet is crazy about Dave—probably because he takes her on such epic walks.

"If you and Mia got married, Will, then Harriet would be our dog, too!"

"You'd like that, wouldn't you, Dave."

"Are you going to marry her, Will? Are you going to have babies?"

"Maybe, Dave. We'll have to wait and see."

"Are you going to have *sex*, Will?"

"If we're going to have babies, it might be necessary, Dave."

According to *The Encyclopedia of Tennis*, "in the Zone" means a state of great confidence, when one is playing sensationally. When you've been going out with a girl for a while, you start to get a whole new respect from people. The girls treat you more seriously, and the guys line up to ask you about girls and what they think. Now, at lunchtime, there's the line for the arm wrestlers, the line for Yorick's chess game, and the line for girl problems, with me as chief consultant.

"What should I get her for her birthday?"

"What movie should we see?"

"What should I *do* on the first date?"

But most of the time my answer is disappointing.

"I don't know about *other* girls," I say. "I just know about Mia."

Mia

So now I have the perfect bedroom, with the perfect boyfriend to go in it. Will comes over to my place and lies on my new bed while I practice my viola. I make him close his eyes, because otherwise he goes all gooey, and it's too hard to concentrate. Will talks about how good things are between us. He wants to get an anchor tattooed on his arm, but I say to him, "Who do you think you are, a sailor?" Things have quieted down at home. Dad comes around to visit, and Mom even lets him in. Dad and Tina aren't together anymore, as far as I know. But Mom has a male nurse friend who she *assures* me isn't gay, so that sounds interesting.

Renata is still in Yugoslavia. Her family has decided to live there. Renata wrote a long, sad letter, addressed to "My two best friends." Vanessa and I cried when we read it. If we could still be best friends with Renata, how hard could it be being friends with each other? Vanessa is okay. You just can't leave her alone with your boyfriend for too long.

Vanessa has had plenty of flings with boys, but she's never actually had a relationship.

"What's your secret?" she asked me the other day.

(That was funny. Vanessa asking *me* about boys.)

I could have said all that stuff about trust and commitment, about not letting go, but giving the guy a bit of slack to let him find things out for himself. I could have talked about respect and compromise. After all, that stuff is important.

Instead, I told Vanessa, "The main thing is, we're not in a hurry. And Will is *such* a good kisser!"